UNDER
THE SHANGHAI
TUNNELS
AND OTHER WEIRD TALES

LEE WIDENER

Under the Shanghai Tunnels was originally published by
Dunhams Manor Press, 2012
At the Shoeshop of Madness was originally published by
Omnium Gatherum Media, 2013
KONG-Tiki was originally published by
Voluted Tales, 2014

I would like to thank Jordan Krall, Emory Barrett Puschell, Kate Jonez and Voluted Tales for originally editing and publishing some of these stories. I would also like to thank Ross Lockhart for inspiring Sleeper Under the Sea, and finally the crew from Stranghouse Books - Nicholas Day, Don Noble and Jeff O'Brien, for making this so easy. And to Jim Agpalza for capturing the essence of Under the Shanghai Tunnels with a single image.

Finally, thanks to my mother and my sister for fostering my love of reading, and for letting me read any damn thing I wanted to.

TABLE OF CONTENTS

UNDER
THE SHANGHAI
TUNNELS
AND OTHER WEIRD TALES

Under the Shanghai Tunnels

It had been overcast all day and around nine o'clock it finally started raining. Big surprise for Portland. It was one of those non-committal Oregon rains; it wasn't a drizzle, and it wasn't a downpour. Just enough rain to make things uncomfortable if you stayed outside. I didn't feel like being uncomfortable so I needed to find a place to be inside.

I had been downtown most of the day searching through the dusty shelves in the back room of Cameron's Books. Leaving at closing time with one magnificent find, the most convenient place to get out of the rain would be Morrises, a faded old bar that still tenaciously clung to a touch of elegance. It refused to be ravaged by age without a fight.

I loved Morrises. It was a little rough around the edges, but it was friendly and full of atmosphere. And then there was Wilson. Wil was my oldest friend and part owner of Morrises. We'd become fast friends in grade school, bonded by a mutual love of books. Even now, years after we'd finished college, we had both come back to Portland, and we were still friends. You could find him there most nights, blowing sax with his trio.

As soon as I stepped through the door I could hear him torturing that poor saxophone. He was making that horn scream. I knew the tune instantly. It was a cover of an old R & B number- "The Party Stomp". Wilson could make a sax sound dirty like nobody else. Melanie's flute screeched and squealed like it was in bed with that saxophone. Jesus, the guitarist, laid out a wall of sound like he WAS the bed, the springs gasping in rhythm with the sexual sonata.

I closed my eyes and I could smell the cigarette smoke and cheap beer, just as if I was in an old road house in the fifties, even though it was now illegal to smoke in a bar. After ordering a brandy, I headed for the music. The side room was alive, jiving in time with the trio of musicians, no evidence of the dreary weather outside. In here was joy and abandonment. Only the moment and the music mattered. No thoughts of the future and the uncertainty it could bring. I caught Wil's eye as I headed for a table in the corner, and he nodded.

Wilson played here almost every weekend and often during the week. He was one of the best saxophone players on the West Coast. *Ebony* had even done a cover story about him. The building had been in his family for generations, and he had a piece of the action. It had originally been a hotel, one of the nicest at the time Portland was originally settled. Now the hotel was long abandoned, parts of the building rented out for storage and studio space, and some of it had long ago fallen into disuse and disrepair.

"My man, my man Melvin, how are you this evening?"

That deep voice was a welcome sound. I looked up to see Wilson smiling at me. He grabbed my hand and gave it a squeeze as he sat down.

"You guys are cooking tonight," I said. "That rendition of 'The Party Stomp' was hot!"

Wilson chuckled. "Thank you, kind sir. What brings you to Morrises tonight?"

"Do I have to have a reason to visit my oldest friend?"

"Of course you don't, but I see you have a package there."

I glanced at the package and grinned.

"Yes, I have been to Cameron's Books, and I have made a discovery. I'm not sure they even knew what they had. They let me go through some boxes from a recent estate sale. It pays to be a good customer."

Carefully I unfolded the paper and slowly drew forth a slim and tattered ledger. The black leather cover was cracked and crumbling. Beaming, I looked over at Wilson. "Isn't it beautiful?"

"What is it you have there?"

As carefully as possible I opened the ragged book to the first page, wrinkled and water stained. I pointed to the smudged words written in ink at the top of the page: Mary's Harbor Lodge, 1852.

Wilson's eyes grew wide and he slid his chair closer.

"Mary's was just down the block from here," he breathed.

We were both fascinated by local history and

9

had spent countless hours researching northwest history, particularly Portland's early days. We even considered ourselves amateur experts. My finger trembled as I drew it down the page to the next words.

Wilson read them aloud. "Cargo Manifest."

His eyes followed my finger down the page.

"January 3rd," he read. "Ephias Dingham, Roberto Santucci. Jan. 5th. Georgie Morton, Willum Foucault." Wilson paused. "It says cargo manifest, but all it lists are men's names."

"Exactly." I smiled. I knew he'd make the connection. Suddenly he drew back, his eyes narrowing.

"The Shanghai Tunnels," he whispered.

"That's right," I said. "This is a record of men who were shanghaied at Mary's in 1852."

"I've never heard of this kind of document before," he said, staring at the book.

"It may be the only one in existence. It shouldn't exist. They didn't keep records of this kind of thing."

"Hey, you guys look pretty serious." It was Melanie, the flute player from Wilson's trio. Her arms circled my neck from behind and she kissed my ear. Her long gray hair fell over my face. The familiar scent of her soap scrubbed skin was still intoxicating. She and I had... history. "Break time's over, Wil," she said as she glided away from the table. "The natives are getting restless."

He gave me a stern look as he stood up. "Don't you go anywhere."

"Don't worry!" I said. "I'm not moving." I spotted my favorite waitress, Jenny, and ordered another brandy, settling in for the next set. Most of the crowd had cleared out and the place had quieted down. When Melanie blew that first beautiful note on her flute, I knew we were in for some jazz. Jesus strummed a chord that immediately made me think of Joe Pass, and when Wilson edged his way into the riff with a subdued arpeggio, it was pure love. The previous set had been primal, dirty, like aural fornication, but this tune was clean, gentle, a declaration of spiritual love. No matter how many times I heard this trio, I was always astounded at the emotion they could create with just the sound of a few notes.

The music and the brandy lulling me into a sense of well-being, I flipped through the ledger to see what other mysteries it might hold. The names themselves evoked mysterious images of countless crimes committed long ago. Portland had once been infamous as a place where unsuspecting individuals often went missing, shanghaied by unscrupulous sea captains, either as crew for their ships, or cargo, as white slaves. This was accomplished through a series of secret underground tunnels connecting several disreputable institutions with the pier on the Willamette River. Unsuspecting individuals were held in cells in the tunnels until it was time to ship them out. During the Depression, long after the practice of shanghaiing had ceased, the tunnels served another purpose- they housed speakeasies. Now the Shanghai Tunnels were a tourist attraction. Weekly tours were given, and participants thrilled to stories of unsavory occurrences in the Portland Underground.

The very existence of the book sent my imagination reeling. I held it close, inhaling the mold, the decay, the age. What age-old tales were trapped within the archaic, smeared script? What mysteries were held within the covers? Lives interrupted, cut short by an ill-timed visit to a darkened saloon, sometimes never to be heard from again.

Slowly turning the water wrinkled pages, the lists of names conjured up images of unfortunate souls lost to friends and family, lost to history.

Bert Akley

Isayah Teachout

Everett McNeil

Washington Morton

Gideon Loveman

And then, ten pages in, under the listing for November 14th, 1852, I saw a name that made my blood freeze. I didn't want to believe what I was reading. Draining my brandy in one gulp, I ordered another. Staring at the page, reading and rereading it, I wondered if my suspicions could possibly be true.

I wanted to get up and leave but I'd have to face Wilson eventually. The music the band was playing was sublime, but focusing on it was impossible. My mind was racing, imagining what Wilson would say when I showed him what I had found. If my suspicions were true, this discovery would affect him deeply.

Applause invaded my reverie. The trio of musicians had finished and were packing up their instruments. I checked my phone for the time and was surprised to see it was 1:30 already. Time flies when you're lost in thought. Wilson was coming my way so I downed the rest of my drink. I needed to steady my nerves for this.

"What did you think, my man?" Wilson asked as he sat across from me, setting his saxophone case on the table.

"Inspiring as always," I replied. Wilson would be making a fortune in any other city but Portland. He loved this city, just as I did. It was part of his being. His family had lived here for generations. They had once been slaves, but had gained their freedom and moved to the fledgling Portland, weaving their history into the city's history.

There would be no way to break it to him gently, so, holding my breath, I simply pushed the book across the table. "Check out the entry for November 14th, 1852."

A waitress deftly sat a coaster and Wilson's standard drink, an Old Fashioned, on the table as the musician reached for the book. He ran his fingers over the worn leather before gently opening the volume, a look of satisfaction on his face. He loved anything old, as did I, but old books were the supreme treasure to us, and if they were rare, that fired our imaginations even more.

I watched as Wilson carefully turned each page, his eyes devouring the lists of evocative names, until he got to page ten. My eyes were riveted on Wilson, waiting for his reaction. He read down the list till he got half way down the page and then the blood drained from his face. Attempting to maintain his composure he carefully placed the book on the table and downed his drink in one stiff gulp. Picking up the book and reading the page again, he turned his gaze on me. I could see the confusion, the disbelief, in his eyes.

"It's got to be," I said.

His hands were shaking, so I took the book

from him, and reread the page again. November 14th, 1852, fourth name in the list: Wilson Davis, my friend's great-great-great-great-great-grandfather.

The story of the first Wilson Davis' disappearance was a legend in their family. He had been out conducting business that night. His wife Sophia and their three children never heard from him again. The family was well off, business owners, but in 1852 the disappearance of one black man was not a high priority case for police – especially in Portland, where people disappeared with an above average frequency.

Portland was an inland port on the banks of the Willamette River. During its infancy, sea captains would sometimes find themselves in need of extra crew members... in a hurry. Supply was always ready to meet demand, and an industry arose to provide able bodies, willing or not, to man outgoing cargo ships. Inquisitive lawmen found themselves well compensated for their silence; or they might disappear themselves.

Wilson stared into space, lost in thought. It was several minutes before he finally spoke.

"Old Wil Davis' disappearance has troubled my family for generations. He was the backbone of our family. He bought his freedom, his wife and children's freedom, became a business owner, a respected man in his community. His example has inspired every generation that came after. You know that our family history is very important to us. Every new generation learns about old man Davis, and why we should be proud of him. But that legend has a dark side, the story of his disappearance. We still talk about it. We have a need to know what happened. My grandfather even hired a detective company once, to look into the matter."

He placed his hand on his saxophone case and ran it back and forth.

"This happened a long time ago, but it continues to affect my family. We lost one of our own. Not just anyone, but the man who we look to as the head of our line. At family gatherings it always comes up; holidays, weddings- somebody will always say it. 'I wonder whatever happened to Old Wil'. It's like none of us has been complete ever since."

I knew Wilson better than I knew anyone else. I could hear the pain in his voice, the loss.

"We have to get to the bottom of this," I said.

He almost smiled, and by the look in his eyes, I could tell that was exactly what he was waiting for me to say. He reached across the table and touched my arm, relieved he wouldn't be trying to solve this mystery alone.

The bartender's voice gave us both a start.

"Closing in fifteen minutes, guys."

"Thanks, Auggie," Wilson said. "Mel, come with me." He lifted his sax from the table and headed for the private offices. I wrapped up the ledger and followed him past the bar and into a seedy office. He set the instrument on a desk and locked the door. Picking up a flashlight, he motioned for me to follow him into a hallway lit only by bare light bulbs hanging from the ceiling on wires. The floorboards creaked as we walked past dusty doorways to a stairway at the end. He flicked on another row of lights and started down the stairs.

"Where are we going?" I asked.

"Just come," was his only reply.

Wilson had taken me prowling through this gigantic building many times, but never into the basement. It smelled damp down there. The painted brick walls were buckled and uneven. Dust was everywhere, thick on the stairs. At the bottom Wilson turned left and I hurried to catch up with him. I didn't want to be left alone down there.

As I followed him into a room on the left I felt like I was in a bombed out bunker in World War II. Beams from the ceiling hung at precarious angles. Floor to ceiling cages made of wooden slats lined the walls. A dented, rusty boiler squatted in the corner. Broken wooden crates were strewn everywhere. Inch-thick dust and debris covered the floor. Another single light bulb somewhere inside the room threw ominous shadows. I could hear Wilson rummaging through things. Something fell over and I just about jumped out of my skin. Cautiously, I stepped forward.

"Are you okay, Wilson?"

"Yes, just some junk falling over."

I picked my way through the detritus of ages long past. A pile of broken bottles was swept against a wall. Half seen forms lurked beneath dusty sheets, piled in the corners. Several broken tables, upended, waited to be set right. A cracked and worn bar ran along a wall.

"What is all this?" I asked, coming up behind Wilson, who was examining a portion of the wall.

"This is where Morrises did business during Prohibition," he answered.

"Why haven't you shown this to me before?"

"I don't come down here much. We kind of keep it closed off so the building inspector won't want to come snooping around down here. A couple of nights ago I was in the office after a show. I was the only one in the building. It was so quiet I was kind of lost in thought. Then I heard a noise. It sounded like something falling, but it was muffled, and it came from somewhere below. I decided to take a look around. I ended up here." He nodded toward the wall.

I looked closer and noticed a portion of the ceiling had fallen, cracking the brick wall and opening a section in the wooden wall next to it. Water trickled through the crack in the wall. A dank stench permeated the air.

"You know how much it's been raining lately," Wilson said. "The weight from the rain, and the decrepit nature of things down here caused the ceiling to collapse and pushed this wall open. Take a look." He shined the flashlight into the opening.

I peered into the opening and beheld something entirely unexpected, terrifying, and wonderful. It was a primitive tunnel, descending into the darkness. The walls were jagged, like they'd been hacked out of the earth and stone with something sharp. Long ago, someone had built a wall, closing off the opening.

"What's down there?" I asked.

"I don't know," Wilson answered. "I haven't explored it yet."

"We have to go down there!"

"Yes, but not yet. When we both have time and are well rested. How's your Wednesday look?"

"It's all yours. Do you think this is part of the Shanghai Tunnels?"

"I don't know," he answered. "My family has always denied having anything to do with all that."

He turned and headed for the exit, for the

surface world, back to present day, and I followed him.

"That could lead to the Shanghai Tunnels. Maybe we can find out something about your ancestor's disappearance," I said.

"Yes, maybe," he said, frowning.

He turned out the light, weaved his way through the debris and headed up the creaking wooden stairs. I looked at the book, which I was still clutching, stuffed it in my coat pocket and hurried after Wilson.

***

The next day, after thoroughly examining my little ledger, I set it in a place of honor in my library of Portland antiquities. Someday I might be able to publish it, shedding some light on a dark part of Portland's history. Wednesday couldn't come soon enough for me, and when it finally got here I was anxious to embark on the forthcoming adventure. Though I was by vocation and avocation intellectually inclined, I believed in leading a well-rounded life, so I had the accouterments necessary for an excursion of this nature.

I equipped my backpack with a length of sturdy nylon rope, a wicked looking camping knife, leather gloves, a flashlight and extra batteries, digital camera, several bottles of water and a supply of energy bars. There might be some rough terrain, so I wore a pair of heavy duty hiking shoes, old jeans and a waterproof jacket. My worn fishing hat completed my outfit. At the last minute I grabbed a couple of flares.

When I got to Morrises, Wilson was waiting for me in the office.

"I've been talking to my family," he said. "Trying to find out if there had ever been any kind of information on what happened to old Wil Davis. Nobody ever heard anything from him after the night he disappeared. It scarred the family, back then. His wife and kids were never the same. My relatives still talk about the mystery." Finally, he looked over my outfit and cracked a smile. "Mel, what are you made up for?"

"Well, I like to be prepared," I chuckled.

"I do too," he replied picking up a battery powered lantern. "Let's get going."

Once again I followed him into the decrepit basement. Even though it was high noon, it felt more like the witching hour down there. Wilson didn't seem like he was in a talkative mood, so I followed him in silence. With every step we seemed to be moving back in time. I wished we could stop and rummage through the debris. Surely there were antiques worth uncovering tucked away in the corners of this subterranean wonderland.

When we got to the back room he set the lantern on the floor and sat down on a broken wooden stool.

"I went to see my granddad yesterday," he said.

"I haven't seen him in years," I replied. "How's he doing?"

"Not so well. He's really getting up there. I asked him if there was any chance Morrises had ever been part of the Shanghai Tunnels. I never saw him get so upset in my life. Gave the old man a conniption fit. I felt like crap afterwards. He asked me how I could even ask such a thing, given our family's history. He was right. Wilson Davis started life as a slave, but he ended it as a free man. He freed his wife and children. The entire Davis family is proud of that accomplishment. Nobody in this family would have anything to do with kidnapping and selling people into servitude." He took a long look at the hole in the wall. "So why is that hole there?"

"Well, your family didn't build this place," I said. "It must have been there when they bought it. It was probably already walled over."

"Probably. But it's still troublesome."

"Come on, man. Light up that lantern. Let's see what's in that tunnel."

Wilson grabbed the lantern and stood up.

"Mel, I'm glad you're here with me."

Smiling, I put my hand on his shoulder.

"You know I wouldn't miss this for anything."

He turned on the lantern and held it up. Adjusting my backpack I peered over his shoulder. The lantern threw a wavering patch of yellow light into the tunnel and then was swallowed by the dark abyss. A rough descending pathway, thick with grit, led down into the unknown past. He stepped down into the tunnel, and I took one last look at the crack in the wall, still damp from rainwater, before following.

We shuffled silently down the path, peering as far into the darkness as we could. It didn't take long before we were overtaken by an eerie sense of isolation. Beyond the feeble circle of light cast by our lantern, the darkness was total. There was nothing behind or in front, neither above nor below; there was only the small spot of existence open to our prying eyes. As we moved downward, the world above us ceased to be. Equally unsettling was the complete lack of any sounds besides those we produced ourselves. Above, in that distant land barely remembered, there was always some kind of background babel- traffic, building noises, music, distant hubbub- always something. Here there was nothing but our breathing and the sounds of our footsteps. Because of the lack of any other sounds, those we produced took on a greater significance. The tunnel was just large enough for the two of us. It's a good thing neither of us was claustrophobic.

***

It also didn't take long for the temperature to drop. The air had become cold and clammy. Downward, ever downward we shuffled, a few inches at a time, looking for who knows what. The walls were free of any kind of adornment, the only variety the jagged marks formed by whatever tool had carved this tunnel. A few turns in direction made it impossible to keep track of where we were in relation to the world above. Each step took us farther into a jet black nothingness, a land of no time, no space, just the eternal now.

"Wilson," I said, my voice a whisper that sounded too loud in this tomb-like silence.

"Hmm."

"How far down do you think we've come? About the level of the Shanghai Tunnels, or farther, or what?"

"I don't know. Hard to say."

"Seems like we should have connected to the tunnels by now. Maybe this goes somewhere else."

We edged around a sharp turn in the stairway

and stopped cold. I put my hand up to cover my nose and mouth. The stench was terrible. It smelled like a septic tank had emptied into a backed up sewer and they both erupted onto the sidewalk.

"Jesus Christ," I said, "What is that?"

Wilson wasn't paying attention. He was bent over, examining something on the floor. As I looked down, he was brushing the dust away from a spot in the pathway. There, etched into the earth was an uneven circle, several inches in diameter, with a thick wiggly line leading away down the path. The circle and line both glistened with some kind of dried substance.

"Wilson, don't you smell that awful stench?" I asked.

"Of course I smell it. It's disgusting. But what do you make of this?"

"I'm not sure about the circular shape, but if I saw a line that looked like that on a sidewalk, I'd say it was a slug trail."

He held the lantern out a little farther down the path. The thick etched line meandered along as far as the light shone, gleaming in the artificial beam. Wilson stood and followed the etched line down the tunnel.

"Christ, Wil, how can you stand that stink?" I asked, following him.

He was moving faster, spurred on by a new purpose. I hurried to catch up. I didn't want to be left by myself in this darkness. A few yards farther down, there were two misshapen circles etched in stone, with two wiggly lines circling them, coated with the hardened luminescent substance. Another couple yards down, another circle joined the thick wavy lines. Every step we took downward now had at least one misshapen circle etched into the stones or earth. Often there were several, and each circular shape had a thick undulating line attached to it. The lines were unending, so the steps were becoming quite cluttered with irregular patterns of lines.

The circles and trails increased the deeper we went. Some circles could be found on the walls, as high as four feet. Wilson was possessed. He held the lantern high and raced down the tunnel. I rushed just to keep up.

"Wilson, slow down!" I implored, and just as I said that the lantern shot off to the right and hit the wall. My friend disappeared from view and the lantern hit the floor with a crash. It threw a ghostly wavering light across the ceiling.

A cry of pain filled the air and I looked down. Wilson was on the floor, his arms splayed out, and he was struggling. I grabbed the lantern and ran over to his side. He had fallen into a hole and was doing his best not to fall all the way in.

"Are you just going to stand there?" Wilson shouted.

Spurred to action, I dropped the lantern and grabbed Wilson around the shoulders. With much grunting and groaning I managed to pull my friend from the hole. We both sat on the floor, catching our breath.

"Are you alright, man?" I asked.

"My ribs hurt like hell, but I don't think I broke anything."

The walls and floor around the hole were covered with hundreds of the wobbly circle impressions and curvy, disjointed lines. The odor was almost unbearable. I lifted the lantern and crawled over to the hole, trying to see what was down there. I couldn't see much with the lantern, so I got the flashlight out of my backpack. Lying on the floor, I stuck the flashlight and my head inside the hole. The flashlight revealed a chamber about a dozen feet deep, twenty feet square. The walls and floor were pockmarked with the same circles and lines. Then I saw something that made me freeze and pull back out of the opening as fast as I could.

I sat gasping, trying to get over the shock of what I'd seen.

"There's a skeleton down there."

It was a moment before Wilson replied.

"What?"

"A skeleton. Human bones."

"Give me that flashlight."

He took the flashlight and pointed it into the chamber.

"He still has some clothes on," Wilson said. "I'm going down there."

"This might be some kind of important find. Shouldn't we get some help? The police, or an archeologist or something?"

"Are you serious? You brought rope, right?"

"Yes." I opened my pack.

"We've been climbing together enough times to do this. You lower me down there and then I can climb out with the rope."

"Wilson, we're not twenty-five years old anymore."

"Shut up and get that rope out."

I knew there was no reasoning with him, so I took out the rope, tied it around my waist and handed him the remainder. He wrapped it around his arms and lowered himself into the dark chamber. I was right to mention we were not the young sprites we'd once been. He'd put on weight and it was all I could do to keep from falling into the hole. Fortunately, he didn't have far to go and he soon reached the bottom.

"Send the lantern down here," he called.

I pulled up the rope, tied the lantern to it and lowered it into the hole. Once he had the lantern, I lay down and peered into the hole. Wilson was standing in the middle of the chamber, holding up the lantern and turning around in a circle.

"The walls are just covered with those circular markings. And there are more bones than this one skeleton."

He took a few steps toward the pile of bones and cloth.

"The markings get more numerous as they get closer to these bones."

Setting the lantern on the floor, he knelt next to the bones and examined the clothes.

"There's something in one of the pockets."

Then he was silent for a long time. Finally, in that utter silence of this nowhere place, I could hear him quietly sobbing.

"What is it?" I asked. "What is it?"

I could see him lay his hand against the side of the skull, in what seemed like a tender gesture.

"Get me out of here," he said, his voice choked with emotion.

He tied the lantern to the rope and I pulled it up. I then lowered the rope back down the hole, braced myself the best I could, and Wilson struggled as he climbed. When he got to the top I grabbed his shirt and pulled him up into the tunnel. Both of us exhausted from the exertion, we sat with our backs against the wall, trying to catch our breath.

After a while I couldn't stand it anymore.

"What is it you saw down there?"

Without a word he reached in his pocket, took out a leather notebook and handed it to me. My hands quivering, I opened the first page. In a tiny, cramped hand, written in pencil, were the words *The diary of Wilson Aaron Davis.*

After a few moments I realized I wasn't breathing. I looked over at my friend. His eyes were closed, and he was scrunched over, almost in a fetal position. I'd seen him like this only a few times in my life. He was doing his best to stave off emotional collapse. I had to get him moving, quick. Handing the book back to Wilson, I gathered all my supplies and put them back in the pack. I realized how dry my throat was, so I took a drink from one of the water bottles.

"Take a drink," I said, handing him the bottle. "Let's go back. We can look at that thing in the light."

This time I carried the lantern and led the way. My thoughts were racing. Could those really be the remains of my friend's ancestor? How could he have ended his days in a chamber deep beneath his own building? I was thankful that the farther we got from that horrible chamber, the better the air smelled.

Thinking aloud, I mumbled "I wonder what these markings are."

There was no response from Wilson. Weary, we trudged up the stairs, our pants covered in the fine dust coating the stairs. We made our way through the basement and back to the office. Glancing out the window I could see it was already nighttime, and it was raining. We had been below a lot longer than I thought. I set the lantern on the desk and turned it off.

"I'm going to get us something to eat and drink," I said.

Walking down the hall to the bar, I could barely believe the day's events.

"Hey, Auggie, how 'bout a couple of burgers, a bottle of Scotch and two glasses," I said to the bartender.

"Well, hi, Melvin," he replied. "I didn't see you come in."

"I got here this morning. Wilson and I have been having a meeting in the back office."

"A meeting, you say?" He took a fresh bottle of Scotch from the bar and put it on a tray with two glasses and a couple of burgers that set my stomach grumbling. Luckily it was Happy Hour and they were just waiting for us. "What kind of meeting?"

"Long story," I said, grabbing the tray and heading back to the office. When I closed the office door behind me, Wilson was sitting at the desk, his head in his hands, the notebook on the desktop.

"Here, eat this," I said, placing a plate with one of the burgers in front of him. "You need it."

I sat across from him, devouring the other burger. I needed the food as much as Wilson did. Aside from the nourishment the sandwiches provided, the very act of eating grounded us, brought us from that nightmare below, to the sanity of the normal world. I cracked open the Scotch and poured two drinks, handing one to Wilson. He took the glass and downed it in one drink. He let out a deep sigh and relaxed. Wilson stared at me as I wolfed down the rest of the burger.

Once I pushed my plate away, he spoke. "You read it to me," he said, handing me the notebook.

"Are you sure?" I asked.

"I got to know, but I can't bear to look at it myself... so you read it out loud."

I poured us both another drink, and we drank them before I picked up the mysterious diary. Could this really be what it purported to be? The brown leather of the cover was worn but intact. Inside, the pages were turning brown and with the tiny, cramped script, it was difficult to read.

The Diary of Wilson Aaron Davis. November, 1852. I pray to my dear Lord in Heaven to deliver me from this Hell I find myself in. In the past several days, I have no way of knowing the exact number, I have seen many things my mind cannot comprehend. I don't know if I can rightly put them down here.

Has it been a day, or more? I barely know. I lost my pocket watch in the struggle. The normal world above ground seems so far away after what has befallen me. Dear God, I surely regret making that ill-fated decision to visit Mary's Harbor Lodge, that iniquitous pit of deceit and Deviltry. I had a bill to collect, and I was sure if I payed her a visit, she would be forthcoming, but when I got there she was drunk, and surly as Lucifer.

As a habit, I try to maintain a cordial demeanor with everyone I have dealings with, but that woman would put the patience of an Angel on trial. A five dollar debt was all I wanted to collect. Five dollars. If I had known it would come to this result, I would have gladly forgiven my claim.

As soon as I set foot in that sinful edifice, that lady, and I use that term politely, she started in a hollerin' and a screaming at me like I was some Unholy Demon come to carry her to Hades. I tried to calm her down, but she just commenced to screeching like a witch putting a curse on my Immortal Soul. I figured there was no use to be served by staying there, so I determined I would just leave. Mary had other ideas for me though, and directed her henchmen to lay hands on me. I tried to reason with them, but they were having none of that, so I did my best to remove myself from their clutches. I laid one of them flat on the floor, but it was no good, there were too many of them.

Give him to the Captain! that harridan shouted, and those thugs dragged me down the stairs and through a wall that opened up. One of them called into the darkness- Are ya there, Captain? Yessir! A voice yelled from somewhere below. We got another one for ya, my captors yelled back, and they threw me into the darkness. I fell head over heels down a wooden set of stairs. Nearly senseless, my bones aching, I heard laughter, and once again hands were laid upon me.

When I could get my eyes open I saw I was being carried down an underground tunnel, filthy with garbage. I knew where I was – the Shanghai Tunnels. Everybody knew about them, but most were lucky enough to never see them. My head was starting to clear. I knew I had to get out of there, but at the moment I was a prisoner. This sent me into a state of despair. I had been a Free Man for more years than not, and I was not going to give up my freedom easily.

They took me down long hallways, turning every which way and that, till I lost all sense of direction. Finally they took me into a room lined with cells. They rifled through my pockets, relieving me of my money, my wallet, my handkerchief, and my genuine Swiss pocket watch, marveling that a darkie had such a fancy timepiece. I was in a dour mood, eying the bars on those cells. I knew what these miscreants had in mind for me. I was being shanghaied. Tomorrow I'd be in the hold of some foul ship, forced into serving as crew.

When they brought out the shackles I'd had enough. I knew the feeling of iron on my ankles from my days as a Slave, and I vowed long ago I'd never know that feeling again. Fueled by desperation I hit the man holding me with every ounce of strength I could muster. I hit him in the stomach and he doubled over. The man with the shackles stared at me like I was a dog who'd eaten his dinner. I didn't waste time. I turned and ran out of that room, and down the tunnel in the direction I hoped was the way we had come.

I ran for all I was worth. There was no way under God's Good Heaven I would let those men catch me. I figured I had to try and find another way out, since if I went back up to Mary's, I'd be in the same trouble once more. So I started feeling the wall for a door or another passageway, or anything. I had to hurry, because my captors would catch up to me soon. My search was soon rewarded, much to my relief. As I inched my way along the wall in the dark, my foot discovered an impression in the wall, at floor level. Bending over and examining the edifice with my hands, I discovered it was a hole, about three feet tall, and it went back into the wall as far as I could reach. I didn't even think twice about crawling into that hole. Whatever was in there, it was likely better than being caught by those men pursuing me. I would find out later how terribly wrong I was.

Crawling on my hands and knees down the tunnel because it was not high enough to stand, I heard my pursuers approach and then move on past my hiding place. That was good. They didn't know where I was. I still had to get out of here somehow, and going back led to possible discovery, so forward I must go. The ground was sloping downward, and to my dismay, I could hear sounds – sounds that seemed to be coming from the very tunnel I found myself within. They sounded far away, but it was disconcerting. The possibility that something else inhabited this tunnel besides me was unwelcome. I also became aware of a growing stench that was decidedly unpleasant. It smelled of sewage and a slaughterhouse on a hot day.

Still, there seemed to be no alternative, so I crawled on and on, impossible to say how far, the strange scrambling sounds growing louder, and the repulsive odor growing stronger. And then the world fell out from underneath me. Without warning I found myself tumbling through the air, head over heels. I had fallen through a hole in the floor and was plummeting towards who knows where. I couldn't help myself- I screamed in terror.

Falling through the emptiness in abject darkness was utterly terrifying. And then it was over. I hit bottom and was knocked unconscious.

My throat was getting dry, so I put the book down and poured myself another drink.Looking over at Wilson, my heart went out to him. He was slumped in his chair, staring out the window at the rain. This was hard for him. The mystery of Old Wilson Davis' disappearance had become legend in their family. To find the ending was so tragic was going to affect every member of his clan. Draining my glass, I poured one for Wil. I pushed it across the desk, and without comment, he took it and drank.

"Keep reading," he said. I could see the pain in his eyes. I knew he was determined to find out the truth, though, so I picked up the notebook and turned the page.

The first thing I was aware of upon awakening was that awful smell. It permeated the air. And then there were the sounds. There was a scrambling sound, like something scuttling across a surface, and there was a clicking sound too. The next thing I became aware of was the throbbing pain in my head. Dear Lord, I hoped I hadn't cracked my skull open. I lifted my hand to my head and felt an unbelievably large bump on the back, and also a sticky wet patch. Running my hand over my skull, I didn't find any cracks. Thank God for that.

Finally, I opened my eyes. To my surprise, I was no longer in the dark. I could see I was in a deep cavern, lit by a feeble green glow. I attempted to sit up but was dissuaded from that activity by a multitude of sharp pains from every corner of my body. The worst pain, however, came from my right leg. I rolled on my side and looked down. Sweet Jesus, below the knee, my leg was bent at a most unlikely angle. It was broken.

I was really in trouble now. Here I lay, deep beneath the surface of the Earth, in Hell as far as I knew, pain wracking every inch of my body, my leg broken. I had no idea where I was or how I could remove myself from this situation. I did know I wasn't going to die here, alone, nobody aware of what had come of me. I had a wife, children, grandchildren, employees who all needed me. I may not be as young and strong as I used to be, but I'd be Damned if it all ended here.

I was lying in a small hollow and all I could see were my immediate surroundings, so I pulled myself up to try and get a better view. The pain was excruciating. I had a hellacious amount of bruises and bumps from my fall and every one of them hurt. Sharp, almost unbearable pains shot through my leg, and up through my entire body every time I tried to move. I wanted to let out with a holler, just to release some of the hurting, but I wasn't sure who might be around, and I didn't want to give myself away. So, I inched up the stones, wincing with every stab of pain from my leg.

When I finally got my head up over the top of the rocks, the sight I saw convinced me I was, in fact, in the bowels of Hell itself. The scene before me made so little sense I was like to consider myself insane. I gaped at what I saw, frozen, uncomprehending, and then everything started to spin. I could hold on no longer. The pain and sheer strangeness before me took their toll. My eyes closed and I slipped into unconsciousness.

I woke up- I know not how much time had passed- convinced I was stuck in some horrible nightmare. What I had seen couldn't be real, but as I now know, it was all too horribly, unbelievably real. I was thrust deep inside a living nightmare. Laying there, my head pounding, my leg throbbing, trying to make sense of things, and not having much luck, I got up to try and get a look see again.I poked my head over the rocks, and there was the same indecipherable scene before me.

What I saw was a cave lit by some unknown sickly green phosphorescence. The ceiling was so high it stretched up and away so I could not see where it was. My Dear God, how far underground had I fallen? The cavern itself was comprised of dirt and stone, and all about the surfaces were scarred by grooves of nonsensical shape and pattern that marred every inch.

But Heavenly Angels Above, it was the cursed abominations crawling throughout the cavern that were making those grooves. Loathsome, besotted, misshapen lumps, hundreds of them, slithering around the cave floor, who knows what hideous purpose in mind. They were roughly circular in shape, and had no appendages that I could see, nor eyes, but they did have an opening on their front side that I surmised served as a mouth of sorts. As they squirmed across the stones their mouths opened and closed, making a terrible clicking noise, followed by a sucking sound. Behind them, as they traveled back and forth, they left a glowing trail of slime. As the slime dried it left a groove etched in the ground. Some of the hideous creatures even crawled up the walls, etching trails as they made their way.

A little ways away from me was a man- well, I call it a man, but it was not truly a human being. It looked vaguely human in that it stood upright on two things that resembled legs and had two stalks that approximated arms, but there were no hands on the ends of those things. Instead there was a trio of wicked orange claws, and Dear Lord, on top of its body, where one would expect to find a head, was a mass of writhing snake-like tentacles, and one long stalk that rose above them that had a disgusting orb atop, with a single blinking eye. The monstrosity held a stone staff, etched with arcane symbols, that it used to guide the globular creatures that strayed from whatever purpose he had in mind for them. The bottom end of the staff, where it touched the creatures was pocked and worn.

Those things, as loathsome and hideous as they were, provided a mere prelude to what was the true horror the cave contained. What I next beheld could only be called a monster, a Demon. I struggle to find words to describe the awful construct I beheld when I looked over the cave. I am a strong man. I have seen bad things. I've seen war and starvation. I've seen how ugly one man can be to another, but I had never seen anything in this world that coincided with that... that... thing. It was bigger than any living entity had a right to be. I have been to the circus and seen an elephant, which they say is the largest creature on land. I have been to the ocean and seen whales, which dwarf even an elephant.

This detestable abomination made even elephant and whale look like toys. It filled nearly half the cavern and was bigger than a house, bigger

35

than a three story hotel. It was the size of a small hillside. A big, bulbous, quivering mass of living flesh unlike anything that should rightly live on this Earth. A Devil, a Demon, sent from the depths of Hell was what it had to be, for science could never explain the existence of this monstrosity.

Though huge and amorphous, it was not without features. In the front was a huge sucking maw, similar to those the smaller wiggling creatures had. Above that, three terrible, malevolent red and black eyes popped out from its loathsome body. Protruding from the amorphous mass at irregular intervals were leathery, multicolored, sinuous arms, tentacles actually, each one pulsating with an infernal energy. The repulsive thing's body itself rippled slowly, some secret internal process causing it to buckle and shudder.

I had to brace myself against the rocks to keep from collapsing in shock yet again. Still, there was one more discovery that revealed the ultimate horror. I was not the only human in this chamber. Human skeletons rose in piles in one corner, bones picked clean in some awful fashion and discarded. That was not what shook my sanity to its very foundation. It was the pit filled with a dozen or so men and women, bound by some fibrous material, awaiting who knew what terrible fate. My God, I knew some of them! There was Angus Mills, who had disappeared without a trace the week before. Some of these doomed souls were passed out, mercifully; others moved as if they were in some kind of trance, picking feebly at the foreign bonds confining them. By My Sweet

Heavenly Father Above, what was this impossible panorama before me? What sinful purpose was being served by this ungodly activity?

I knew if I stayed in this diabolical chamber I'd be the next in that throng, so I turned hurriedly to take flight, and that was my undoing. I wrenched my broken leg with that action and I could not stay the pain. I let out a sharp scream and fell to the floor, gripping my leg. That was when that thing- that half-man half thing saw me. It scuttled across the floor to my side, grabbing my arm in one of its powerful pincers. Holy Mother of Jesus he was like to break my arm with that thing!

Who? Who? Who? The words came unbidden into my mind. I didn't hear them proper, they just came into my mind, like a thought- but I wasn't thinking it! I could do nothing but cower on the floor, slack jawed, staring at this not quite man. Again, the thoughts came into my mind. *Who? Who?*

"I'm Wilson Aaron Davis," I said aloud. "Who the Devil are you?"

More words invaded my thoughts, or rather sounds, sounds so garbled, so jumbled, so foreign to my tongue I could never hope to pronounce them, let alone set them down here. I got the feeling it was this thing's name, and since I haven't a hope in Heaven of spelling that sound, I'll just call the thing Crazy Man, for that's what it looked like to me, some sort of crazy manlike atrocity.

Come, it thought to me, and it tugged on my arm with that pincer. I sure wasn't going to get tied up in that crowd, so I tried to yank myself free, but Crazy Man's grip was too tight. It was like being held in a vise.

"I ain't going over there," I said. "Let me go!"

Must come, it said/thought to me.

"No," I said. "You tell me what in God's Name is going on here."

That must have angered Crazy Man because then and there he hit me in the face with that staff. I put my arms up to ward off more blows, but more words came into my mind. *I EXPLAIN. Then you come. You understand planet?*

"Yes, by God, I know what a planet is. We're on one. I been to school. I'm an educated man."

And then came flooding into my mind a plethora of images the likes of which I could never imagine on my own. That thing, that Crazy Man, was showing me its story. It was like a magic lantern show but made up of moving images of the most sophisticated artwork Indeed, they had the appearance not of artwork, but of reality- a reality so far removed from what we call life on this Earth, it might just as well have been from the mind of a drug addled opium smoker.

Crazy Man showed me a world so different from this Earth I had to wonder how it could exist. I saw scenes of a land so dark it was like a nighttime nightmare every day and night. Terrible dark clouds choked the sky and volcanic mountains that reached far into the atmosphere belched clouds of gasses. There was no plant life to be seen. Everything was rocky and jagged. Sulfurous rivers ran through the lands, boiling and bubbling.

There was life on this Hellish place, if life it could be called. Gigantic snake-like horrors swam in the boiling rivers. Wispy, cloudlike forms with faces and limbs floated in the air. On the ground a multitude of ungodly figures slithered, crawled and stalked. There were gigantic pyramid shaped beings with hundreds of legs that moved slowly about the land, as well as vaguely fish-like contrivances running about on four legs.

There were cities too- tall buildings of spires and domes. Ugly slug creatures like those I saw here in this cave paraded in and out of the buildings, engaged in some nefarious purpose of which I knew nothing. Inside one of those buildings was a gigantic tentacled blob creature, the same as the one in front of me. It sat before a monstrous machine of some kind, formed of crystal and metals, manipulating dials and levers, working some evil spell.

The moving images swam through my mind showing me life on this Hellish planet. Months, years, ages passed, I have no idea of the actual length of time. Somehow these creatures formed enormous bubbles made of nothing but light, wrapping themselves and many other creatures in the light. Each of these buildings had its own light bubble inside, and one by one they began to glow with some infernal purpose. They pulsed brighter and brighter, until they seemed afire with the brilliance of a thousand suns. And then they faded away. They didn't get dark... they disappeared, and then they reappeared on distant planets spread throughout the Heavens. What Devilish magic they used to accomplish this, I cannot even guess. It is beyond my ability to fathom. Thousands of these light bubbles traveled to thousands of planets.

Some of these grotesque ships entered our atmosphere, crashing into the sea, the land, the mountains, the desert, burying themselves deep below the surface, sleeping, waiting. This had happened eons ago, and now the inhabitants of those ships were awakening.

Finally the maddening images faded from my vision and I was brought back to my own unfortunate reality. I tried to make sense of the unbelievable spectacle I had been shown. That bizarre creature that was not really a man stood above me.

"Why?" I asked him. "Why have you Demons come here?"

NEED was the word that came into my mind. ROOM. No more space. Here we can GROW.

"I think there might be a few people that have objections to that plan."

NO MATTER. We will grow.

"You can't just show up here and think you can take God's Good Earth away from us."

TAKE AWAY? We here long before your kind. We wait. Now we awake.

"You'll find people are not just going to turn this world over to you so easily. God will protect us and save us from Demons and Devils like you."

GOD? What is god? There is no god. On many planets we are the gods. It will be here too. You are fit only to nourish us.

"Nourish you? You mean-?"

I looked over at that group of poor souls and realized their fate. They were to be fed to those slug things. I would be Damned to Hell if that was going to happen to me. I didn't care if I had to rip my arm off to get loose from this thing, I was not going to end my days as slug bait. Itwisted my body back and forth as hard as I could.

ENOUGH came the thought in my head, so loud I thought my head would explode. Crazy Man hit me with that staff again, and I went down. He drug me across the cave like I was a rag doll. In moments I was wrapped up in a sticky ropelike substance, along with a dozen other unfortunate souls. Crazy Man went back to herding those ugly slug creatures. The deplorable soul next to me was awake, mumbling to himself.

"Brother," I said to him, "How did you find yourself in this Hellish punishment?"

He made no attempt to answer my question, but kept muttering pathetically to himself.

"I said Brother!" I called, louder. He still answered not, so I kicked him as hard as I was able. That seemed to wake him up.

"What?" he said, staring into space.

"Over here, Brother!"

He turned in my direction, his eyes dull, uncomprehending.

"Who's there?" he asked.

"Somebody in the same wretched position as yourself. How did you get here?"

He was silent for a long moment, and then finally answered "I went to Mary's and those bastards shanghaied me. I escaped and got lost in the tunnels. That hateful thing with the club found me."

"What's going on here?" I queried.

Again, he was silent for a long time. At last he answered.

"I barely want to say. It's terrible. One by one we're taken somewhere else. Then there are horrible screams that last for hours, days. Then they take another one. Nobody ever comes back.

Occasionally somebody new joins the queue."

He closed his eyes and took back to mumbling. I struggled like all get out to set myself free from those ropes, but they were made of some kind of strange material I'd never seen before and the more I tried to get loose, the tighter they got. They got so tight I could barely breathe, so I had to stop. I don't know, but I might say those ropes were somehow alive, because they seemed to be breathing when I took a moment to watch them. Between the constant throbbing of my leg, exhaustion, and sheer mental strain, I gave up my fight with consciousness and passed out again.

I have no idea how long it was before I woke up, but when I did, the man who had been next to me was gone. From down one of the many corridors I heard screaming, a man's screams, and it was the most horrible sound I've ever heard a person make. I've heard the terrible sounds of a man having his leg sawn off, after a battlefield injury, and that was enough to give me nightmares for a week, but this was worse. My Lord, I have to admit I wanted to die right then and there. I didn't want to go through what that poor soul was experiencing, and I saw no means of escape.

I took to looking around my surroundings, though truth be told, I didn't much want to see the terrible things this chamber of terrors held. That immense, bloated blob thing wiggled its tendrils and peered about with its three crimson eyes, its sucking maw making repugnant noises. At one point it spit out a spherical object about the size of a cannon ball. Crazy Man was there and used his stick to push it into a pool of foul brackish liquid, where a number of other spheres also floated. There was another, larger pool of fetid liquid nearby wherein what seemed like a hundred of the gross slug creatures lolled about, rolling over and over, writhing and wallowing, intertwining their bodies with each other. I averted my eyes because this activity seemed somehow unholy, unclean. It made my stomach churn.

Elsewhere in the cavern the globlike creatures were attached to the wall in groups. They would pump their bodies up and down a few times, and then rest in place. Afterwards they would move, leaving a dollop of the green luminescent substance behind. In a few minutes a foul stench would fill the air and the green goo would dissolve the stone or earth beneath it, before drying. Another slug would come from behind and do the same thing again, making the impression deeper. Once the smaller lumpy blobs had a hole started, larger specimens followed and carved the holes bigger with their razor sharp teeth. In this manner they were excavating new tunnels. Holy Mother of Angels... if this continued, they'd dig their way to the surface!

I was getting seriously weak. I hadn't eaten in who knows how long, and my leg was a source of constant pain. I was half out my head delirious, lapsing in and out of consciousness, watching these things go through their accursed routines, wondering when my turn would come to travel down that tunnel and meet my maker. I prayed for deliverance. I prayed for my soul to be saved from this torture.

My prayers were not answered, for soon it was my time to take the journey down that frightful tunnel. Crazy Man, his repellent mass of tentacles waving ominously, came and pinched the living rope holding me in place, and it released me. I collapsed on the cavern floor, gulping air, breathing freely for the first time in days, maybe weeks. Who knows?

UP it said in my mind, get up, and to emphasize its point it hit me with its staff. I did my best to stand up, but it was difficult. My right leg was useless- worse than useless, for every time I put any weight on it, searing pain would shoot through my entire body. I rose and stood there, trying to acclimate myself to standing again after so long a time in bondage. Crazy Man hit me across my back and shouted into my mind. GO. I gritted my teeth and limped forward.

I cast a last look at the doomed souls still bound, waiting their turn for oblivion. None of them even noticed my departure. I couldn't fault them. They had long ago given up hope and retreated from their surroundings, their minds vacant, their spirits broken.

The jagged, Hellish orifice loomed in front of me like a giant hungry mouth, waiting to swallow me, swallow my life. The not really a man hit me again. GO. I stepped into the tunnel. It was etched, top, bottom and sides with those lines and circles the slug-things made, and it glowed pale green from the dried residue they left behind. Those hideous crawling creatures clogged the tunnel, and I did my best to limp along avoiding their touch. The odor they produced made me want to vomit. Though they had no eyes, each seemed consumed by their own purpose. A few would stop their activity when I approached and reach toward me with their frightful sucking maws, but Crazy Man would shoo them away with his stick.

We trundled down these corridors, which I now knew had been excavated out of the bedrock by these slug-things. They were in the process of expanding the series of interlocked caves, chambers and tunnels. My embattled mind envisioned a day when the entire Earth was riddled with tunnels, these Beasts of Satan devouring humanity, until there were no people left. The half man half monster would indicate which branch we were to take whenever we came to a junction, and we turned and twisted so many times, if I had not already been hopelessly lost, I would have become so.

Finally we came to a corridor that had a hole in the floor. Dog-sized slug creatures dotted the tunnel, digging new holes, or slithering along on some nefarious purpose. I stood there, looking down into the hole, a feeble green glow barely illuminating the edifice. I turned to ask Crazy Man what I was supposed to do, and he used that staff of his to give me a sharp push. I wasn't prepared, and tumbled backward, falling until I hit the bottom of the hole, striking my head against something hard. Once again, I passed out.

When I woke up, my head hurt like the Dickens. It took a minute to remember where I was, but looking at that hole in the ceiling above me brought it all back. I took a look around. I was laying in a roughly circular chamber about twenty feet across and a dozen feet tall. The walls and floor were covered with the irregular lines and circle shapes, and smeared with the dried glowing green residue. This chamber had been hollowed out by those slug-things. Then I noticed there was an indentation in the floor, containing some weird glowing objects. I went closer to examine them and discovered a dozen or so spheres, about the size of a baseball, glowing with that same infernal light. They were identical to the one I had seen the colossal monstrosity in the cavern spit out. I put my hand close and could feel heat. Something told me these objects were alive. There were also bones littering the floor, and bits of clothing. A few haunted skulls stared up at me from the ground. Oh, Holy Jesus, there was no doubt I was going to die here.

I went to the far end of the chamber and sat down to think, keeping an eye on that cache of disquieting spheres. I spent long hours just staring at that frightful collection, wondering what it might be, and what was going to happen to me down here in this pit. Crazy Man was gone, and none of the slug-things ventured into my prison. I spent a goodly amount of time once again in prayer. I prayed for the Lord Above to bring this entire underground fright house to collapse upon itself, and if not that, at least to end my miserable existence. Please God, I've lived a good life, let me come to Heaven.

Eventually, when I could pray no longer, and the weird balls seemed to be of no immediate danger, I remembered, being a man of foresight and planning, that I always traveled with a notebook and pencil, should there be any need to conduct business with someone I chanced to meet. I felt inside my coat pocket, and to my surprise, my notebook had escaped both the examination of my kidnappers above, and the ravages of my *experiences below ground. I took out my notebook and pencil and began to write this journal. Whoever will see these words, if anyone, I have no idea, but I must set them down. Someone must know what's going on under the Shanghai Tunnels.*

***

I put the book down on the desk. My throat was dry, my emotions were spent, and I needed a drink before I went on. Looking at my watch, I saw it was nearly two in the morning.

"Wilson," I pleaded, "Let's give this a rest. It's crazy."

My friend looked at me with an intensity I'd never seen before. There was anger in his eyes, and he snapped at me.

"Read the damn book!"

"Wilson, come on. It's outrageous."

"You know how important this story is to me, to my entire family."

"Of course, Wil, but it's unbelievable. Your poor ancestor obviously went mad. He fell down into a hole after escaping from his kidnappers and died in that hole, recording the insane ramblings of a poor man who lost hope of ever seeing the light of day again."

Davis stood up with such a force he knocked over his chair.

"How can you say that about Wilson Aaron Davis? He was an educated man, a businessman, dedicated to his family." There were tears in his eyes.

"Wil, no disrespect intended. Anyone would

47

snap in that situation. Who knows how long he spent trapped in that hole?"

"Old Wilson Davis did not go insane."

My friend was breathing heavily and I thought he was going to knock me down.

"Are you going to finish reading that book or not?"

"Well, sure, Wil, but I need a little break. It's nearly two AM."

Wilson grabbed the notebook from the table.

"*Fine.* I'll finish it."

He sat back in the chair and began reading the book aloud. His voice was heavy with emotion. I wasn't sure he'd be able to finish. I sat down and poured myself a stiff drink.

"I must have spent a few days at least, setting down these words," Wilson read. *"I wanted to make sure I left nothing out. If anyone finds this book, they must know every detail."*

Wilson paused and looked at me. "He sounds lucid to me," he said. I knew enough to keep quiet. He continued reading.

After what seemed like ages of writing, sleeping, listening to those creatures in the corridor above slurping and clacking on their insidious business, watching the glowing balls, watching and waiting, for God knows what, something happened. One of those balls changed. A crack appeared in the side, and it kept getting bigger, and bigger, until finally a tiny body appeared, and crawled out of the... egg... for egg it was. It dropped to the ground and sat there, pulsing with its own evil green glow, and then began wriggling across the floor. It was one of those slug-things, a baby, the smallest I had yet seen. It was about the size of a mouse.

As this new awful thing fumbled about on the ground, a crack appeared in another of the eggs, or whatever those spheres were. Soon there were two mouse sized slug-things wandering around the chamber. I watched them, horrified, sitting as still as possible, hoping against hope they wouldn't discover me.

Of course my hopes were in vain. I watched as the tiny wobbly hatchlings turned their maws in my direction and crept slowly closer and closer. I scooted away, but they were on to me and adjusted their course to follow me. There was, of course, no escape. The hole in the ceiling was unreachable, and there were no tunnels leading out. There was no shelter at all. My thoughts turned to self-defense. There was nothing in the chamber that could be used as a weapon, save the bones of previous inhabitants. I am not a superstitious man, but I did not relish the thought of using a dead man's bones to defend myself. Saying a short prayer I bent over and grabbed a bone that looked like it could do some damage. It must have been from an arm or a leg. I crouched against the wall, my macabre weapon raised, watching as those two abominations wriggled across the ground toward me, their hideous sucking maws opening and closing hungrily. As soon as one of the Hellish things came close enough, I brought down my weapon with all the force I could muster.

I've butchered more than a few animals in my day, and I know what the innards feel like. That's exactly what I thought of when my bone club made contact. There was a sickening squish and the baby slug-thing flattened out, but it wasn't more than a few seconds before it was back up and wriggling towards me again. I hit those awful bogies again and again, but I didn't seem to be doing any damage.

I kept scooting back and those things kept coming at me. I had to get away. Using the bone as a crutch, I stood up and hobbled across the chamber, finding myself next to the pit housing the eggs. Glancing down, I noticed four of the spheres were cracked open. Somewhere in this chamber, two more of those fiends were lurking. They soon made their presence known, wriggling out of the pit and dropping to the floor.

I was starting to panic. These depraved creations were multiplying. I was wearing a good sturdy pair of boots. Maybe I could crush the life out of these things. My bad leg would make it difficult to get any leverage, but with my bone crutch, maybe I could pull it off. Steadying myself with the bone, I brought my boot down on top of one of those slug-things, put my full weight on it, and ground my boot back and forth, doing my best to smash the life out of the pitiful creature. I heard a squishing noise, and kept on smashing the blight with my boot. After what seemed like a full minute I took my foot away, to see what kind of damage I'd done. To my surprise I found the bottom of my boot smoking. I lifted my foot and found that my boot had been dissolved where it had come in contact with the improbable malformation. No wonder Crazy Man always avoided touching those things. On the floor the squashed bug started wiggling toward me. Could anything kill these things?

We played this cat and mouse game for some time. I would hobble away from the things, the best I could, and they would track me down somehow and head in my direction again. When they got close I'd use my crutch to slap them away. They seemed tireless, which I decidedly was not. My poor leg kept sending stabbing pains up through my body, no matter how much I tried to protect it. On top of that I was tired and hungry. I couldn't keep this up forever.

That moment of resignation came sooner than I thought. I had to rest, if even for only a few moments. I picked a spot as far away from the horrid crawling shrews as I could get, and sank to the floor. I couldn't move another inch. I was dead tired. Not knowing what fate might befall me, I let my eyes close, another prayer to the Lord on my lips.

I was awakened by that sucking noise. It was close. Too close- when I opened my eyes I saw the malignant creatures were on my boot, wriggling and writhing most unpleasantly. I shook my foot and dislodged two of them. I used the bone to pry the other two off, and what I saw shocked me. There were holes in my boot. They had been eating it.

I hoisted myself to a standing position and limped to another spot as far away from them as I could get. But how long before they found me again? It didn't matter, for I simply had to rest. I slid to the floor again, and as soon as my eyes closed I found sweet oblivion. This time I woke up with sharp slicing, jabbing pains in my right foot. There were six of those creatures now, and they had eaten clear through my boot, and were attacking my foot. The pain and the sheer shock of the sight did me in. I could hold back no

longer and let forth with a scream. I screamed
loud and long, not just from the pain, but from
the despair and rage I felt. What sins had I
committed, dear Lord, for you to deliver me into
Hell this way? I screamed until my voice gave out,
and then I began to cry. Those Demons were
eating me alive.

And then, not due to any action on my part,
one by one, those things dropped from my flesh.
They hit the floor and wiggled away. They must
have had their fill, I figured. I didn't want to, but I
looked down at my right foot. The sight made my
head swim. Still, I had to keep my wits about me.
The flesh on my foot had been half eaten away,
exposing bone and sinew. I wept for the sheer
hopelessness of my position. How long would my
respite be? How long before these things hungered
again? Dare I sleep? Not yet. I took out my
notebook and set down more of my story before
falling into a dreamless slumber, unable to write
another word.

When I woke up, there they were, ringed in a
semi-circle around me, just... waiting. A couple of
them looked larger than when they had first
hatched. I wrote in my notebook. I slept. I watched
the infernal things. Who knows how long this
went on. Eventually they started moving again.
Coming for me, their hunger pushing them
toward me. I didn't bother to fight them off, or try
to escape. What was the use? In the end, they'd
wear me out. God had given up on me, why
shouldn't I?

Once again they found my foot and swarmed
over it. I closed my eyes, for I had no desire to
watch myself being devoured. I could feel tiny,

razor sharp teeth ripping pieces of flesh from my foot, burrowing deeper to slice off muscle and sinew; felt them sucking up my blood as it spurted from my wounds. I could also feel that ooze burning into my skin, dissolving whatever it touched. I screamed again, and wept too, out of pity for my poor, forsaken soul.

For anyone who might read this diary, I will spare you the details of what came next, the endless cycle of those monstrosities feasting on my flesh till they were gorged, the slight respite I got when they rested, allowing me to set things down in this journal and catch some fitful sleep, and then the whole thing repeating again and again. And the pain, the ever present pain, as they chewed my flesh to pieces, and then left open wounds to fester, until their next vile repast They worked their way up my legs, till there was nothing left from the knees down but bare bone. They were growing, too. The first two hatchlings were now as big as a cat, and spent some of their time climbing the walls. All the infernal Devils had been hatched by now, and at times I had a dozen of those things making a meal of me.

As the things grew larger they paid less attention to me, and spent more time exploring the chamber, even climbing the walls. Eventually a few got so large, bloated on my own flesh and blood, that they gained the strength to climb the walls and exit the chamber through the hole at the top. Was this real, or was I, in fact, trapped in some mad delirium? Was I living this Hellish existence, or was it some Devil spawned trial? It mattered little, for this torture was real, and all that mattered.

***

My friends, I have little life left in me. These despicable creatures, invaders on this world from a land so far away I have no idea how to measure it, have completely consumed my legs. I know I have little time left amongst the living. My God has forsaken me, left me to these Demons, to die in Hell, far below the world I've known and loved my entire life. I am weak, so weak, not only from lack of nutrition, but from loss of blood, and from the sheer fact I'm being eaten, inch by inch, by things that should not even exist.

To my dear wife Sophie, and my children Tucker, Wilkie and Sarafina, and all their children, I most desperately beg your forgiveness. I have tried to be the best husband, father, provider, and friend I could be. I have failed you all. Pray for my soul, I beg of you. And pray for this world, for if these things I have seen, and now torment me, have their way, I fear life as we know it will cease to be. This will be the last time I set words down in this book. I barely have the strength to hold this pencil. I will close my eyes one last time and let these devil-spawn finish me off. I'll not pray for salvation any more, for I know my God, if He even exists, which I have come to doubt, has seen fit to punish me for some reason only He can fathom. I say Damn you God, Damn you to Hell, for that is what you have done to me.

***

"That's all there is," Wilson said, setting down

the book. He took out a handkerchief, put it to his eyes, and began sobbing. It seemed like a lifetime of tears came and wouldn't stop. I'd been through trying times with this man. I sat by his side at his Granny Addie's funeral. I was there when his dog was hit by a careless driver. He shed tears on both of those occasions, but nothing like this. I couldn't stand seeing him like this. I rose and put my hand on his shoulder, and did my best to comfort him, but at this moment it meant nothing. I found myself weeping too. Whether this story was true or not didn't matter. Wilson Aaron Davis had died alone, in a pit deep in the Earth, and that was reason enough to mourn.

After a time I poured him a drink and put it in his hand. He downed it in one gulp. He dried his eyes and seemed a little better. I had to try and reason with him.

"Wil, you know I'm here for you no matter what. But think about it. The things in this book, they're crazy. It can't be real. It's terrible, the way he spent his last days, but it was alone, out of his mind. He went mad, mad from grief and loneliness."

He turned to me, his hand gripping the glass so tightly I thought it would break. A quiet, soft spoken man normally, he shouted. "Old Wilson Davis did not go mad! He was a sober, God-fearing man. He was respected. He was the paterfamilias of our line. By every story I've heard about him, he was not given to flights of fancy. Every word in that book is true."

"Think about it, Wilson. Alien slugs living in a hidden complex of tunnels under downtown Portland, eating people alive? It's ludicrous."

"If Wilson Davis the First took the trouble to write it all down before he died, it's true, and there's one way to find out."

I stared at him in disbelief. I knew exactly what he was thinking. "Alright Wil, we'll go down there again, and see what we can find."

He smiled and let out a deep sigh. "Thank you, my man, for sticking by me."

"Not now though. We need to get some rest, be ready for whatever we may find. How about five this evening?"

"That sounds fine. I'll be here, waiting for you."

***

I knew I wouldn't get much sleep, but I had to try. The events of the past twenty-four hours were... well, to put it honestly, they were unbelievable. I couldn't stop myself from running them through my mind, over and over again. Was there any chance at all that the events portrayed in Old Wilson's notebook were true? Of course not. The old man had gone stark raving mad from a combination of pain, hunger, isolation and despair. Anyone would break under those circumstances. I had to try and convince Wilson there was no shame in this. Finally, even my brain was exhausted, and I fell into a fitful slumber.

***

I woke up, hours later, groggy, my limbs aching. Traipsing around those tunnels had taken more of a toll on me than I thought. It was already three o'clock. I ate a quick meal, grabbed my supplies from our last excursion, and headed for Morrises. Walking into the bar, I didn't see Wilson.

"Hey Auggie- have you seen Wil?" I asked the bartender.

"I saw Mr. Davis hours ago," he replied. "He was headed for the office. That's the last I saw of him."

I went back to the office. It was empty. The notebook was there on the desk, where we left it in the wee hours of the morning. The lantern was gone. I knew immediately what was going on. I should have expected it. Wilson was down in the cave already. Had he even gotten any rest, or did he head back into the cave as soon as I left?

I shouldered my pack and headed for the basement, cursing my friend's reckless decision. I wondered how much of a head start he had on me. Anything could happen. He could fall into another hole. Who knows how stable those tunnels were? They could collapse any minute.

There was no trace of him in the basement, so I ventured into the tunnel, calling his name. I eyed the grooves on the tunnel walls as I descended. Could they possibly have been carved from the earth by giant alien slugs? It wasn't even worth considering. I continued calling his name as I crept forward, my voice echoing in the eerie stillness. Irregular circular indentations pocked the walls and floor, the deeper I went, and Old Wilson's fantastic explanation for their presence haunted my imagination.

"Wil? Are you down here?" I called into the darkness.

I got no answer, so I continued down the tunnel, deeper, ever deeper. I was better able to gauge depth this trip, and I was certain I was well below the Shanghai Tunnels. My flashlight, even though it was a decent size, did not give me as large a field of vision as Wilson's lantern had. It was a little disconcerting. I was in constant fear of falling into a hole. The darkness seemed to swallow me up, every step I took.

Finally, I came to the hole in the floor Wilson had fallen into on our first excursion. I shined my beam down into the chamber, illuminating the skeleton of Wilson's ancestor. Such a tragic ending to a strong, upstanding man. But where was Wilson? I focused my light down the tunnel. No trace of my friend.

"Wilson?" I called, suddenly feeling very isolated, deep underground in a corridor that had so many mysteries associated with it. It clearly was not part of the Shanghai Tunnels. So, who made it? With no other alternative, I set out down the tunnel, carefully shining my beam on the floor and walls as I walked. It was a good thing I did, too, for not more than twenty yards down the corridor I discovered another hole in the ground. I cast my light down the hole, and there inside were more human bones.

This wasn't a good sign. Two holes, twenty yards apart, both containing human remains. And all around, both in the holes and in the corridor, those eerie markings. This was starting to look like it wasn't as much of a chance occurrence as I thought. Twenty yards farther on, another chamber in the floor, with more bones inside, another twenty yards and another hole, more bones. It was certain – these chambers had been dug specifically for the purpose of imprisoning people, and those people died there. But, who dug them, who imprisoned people therein, and why? And who were the prisoners? The answers to these questions were inconceivable. In confusion and urgency, I broke the silence once more.

"Wilson! Where are you?"

Farther down the corridor I was presented with another challenge. There was a fork. I almost gave up hope then and there, but shining the flashlight across the floor, I noticed something small in the entrance to the left path. I picked it up. It was a small piece of cane wood. I knew exactly what it was- a saxophone reed. Wilson always carried a few in his pockets. He was leaving me a trail. I headed down the tunnel.

"Wilson! Are you down here?"

Down this tunnel were more chambers and more bones. At the end, more openings to more tunnels, and in one of them, a pen. Another sign from Wilson. This went on for hours. Endless tunnels, some with sunken chambers littered with bones, some without. All of them scored with the maddening lattice of lines and bumpy circles. The ever present stench was getting stronger, but there was still no trace of Wilson, save for the mementos he left at the tunnel openings; a business card, a handkerchief, a dollar bill. I was glad he left these markers, for there was no way of retracing my steps without them. The markers switched from random items to bits of fabric after a while. He'd run out of things in his pockets and was ripping up his clothes. This was something I took note of. Wilson Davis was nothing, if not fashionable. He must feel desperate to be ripping his clothes to shreds.

All the time, the horrible odor that permeated

this network of tunnels was getting stronger, and there were a few times I thought I would have to turn back, it was so strong. Thank goodness I had a strong stomach. And then, finally, one of the tunnels didn't end in more tunnels, it opened into an immense cavern, so big my flashlight beam couldn't reach to the other side. Neither could I see how high it rose. My light just shined into darkness. I stepped into the cave, amazed at the size. It took my breath away. I'd been in caves before, but nothing that matched this. Every inch seemed to be covered by those strange etchings, and there were bones here too.

I wandered about the cave, marveling at my discoveries, tripping over human skulls. The stench here was nearly overpowering, even for me. My mind was overwhelmed, trying to make sense of everything.

"Wilson!" I called. "Wilson!"

This time I was answered by a faint moan, and it came from somewhere inside this cavern!

"Wil!" I cried. "Where are you?"

I heard a grunt and a scuffle and trained my beam in its direction. Halfway across the cave was my friend, lying on the ground. Checking the path between us for holes, I rushed to his side. He was trying to sit up, so I bent down to help him.

"Wil, what happened? Where's your lantern?"

"Broke," he mumbled. He shifted to one side and cried out in pain.

"What is it?" I asked.

He moved his left hand into the light. The three bottom fingers were bent and withered, oozing a greenish puss.

"My God, what happened?"

He gestured to an area behind and above us. I turned the flashlight around and pointed it upwards. I couldn't make out what it was at first. Something big, really big. I played my flashlight left and right, trying to get a better picture of what I was looking at. It was a huge irregular form of some kind, like a big hot air balloon that was half deflated, but there were protuberances- long branch-like things coming out of it that were mottled with different colored patterns. On one end was an opening, a big round hole with jagged edges all around it. Above the hole were three large bumps, and as I trained the light on it, I swear, by all that I know to be true, the closest bump slowly opened up, revealing an obscene approximation of an eye, red rimmed, with an ebony pupil vaguely star shaped. And as I stood there watching it, it rotated and looked straight at *me.*

Every inch of my body came alive with fear, and I wanted nothing more than to run, but my limbs wouldn't move. I was frozen. Then it hit me. It was true. Every goddamn word Old Wilson Davis wrote in that insane diary of his was true. This was that hideous gigantic creature he described, and by God, *it was somehow still alive.* I managed to utter an entirely inadequate epithet.

"Holy crap. How did that thing do that to your hand?"

"I touched one of the tendrils."

Grabbing Wilson under one of his arms, I lifted him to his feet. "We have to get out of here."

We stumbled around the cave for a few minutes, but we finally found the right exit. Wilson had placed a scrap of his t-shirt in front of it. We ran through those tunnels as if our lives depended on it, and they may well have, pausing at the intersections to find Wilson's markers, and running in the right direction, always taking care not to fall in the holes.

"That thing... was alive," I sputtered as we ran. "Jesus, Wilson, *it looked at me.*"

"Apologize," he said.

"Apologize? For what?"

"Apologize, for what you said about Old Wilson Davis."

"Shit, are you kidding me? Yes, yes, I apologize. He wasn't insane. Every word he wrote was true. I still don't quite understand, but the evidence appears to be in his favor."

We said nothing more until we were safely inside Wilson's office. Examining his wounded hand, it was clear that was the priority. I called a cab and we went to the emergency room. The doctors were nosy, as this injury was unlike anything they'd ever seen before. We made up a story about a chemical burn, and stuck with that. They got the wound to stop oozing, but his fingers never recovered. Once we got back to Morrises, there was time to talk in the calming light of incandescent light bulbs, doubt crossed my mind.

"I don't know," I said. "That could have been a giant sculpture, or something, that we saw down there."

"No, I touched it. It was not stone, or wood, or plastic, or anything fashioned by man. It was flesh. What I touched was flesh." He held up his bandaged hand. "Can a statue do this?"

"Okay, so it's real. What are we going to do?" I asked him. "This is huge. I mean, this changes everything that people know. What do we do?"

"We aren't going to do anything."

"What do you mean? There's an alien being down there, and it's *alive*. We have to do something!"

"It's been down there for at least a hundred and sixty years, and who knows how long before that, yet it hasn't done anything."

I couldn't believe what I was hearing. "What if somebody finds it?"

"Nobody's found it yet."

"But what if they do?"

"If that happens, then we can deal with it. But think about this, Mel. In Old Wilson's diary he described the creature as the size of a hillside. Something that dwarfed elephants and whales. The thing we glimpsed down there was nowhere that big. Either he exaggerated quite a bit, or that thing has shrunk. A lot. I think it's dying."

I thought for a minute. "That sounds logical."

"Let me have my way on this, Mel. This involves my family, and Morrises. I don't want that can of worms opened up. I went down there to see if I could find out what happened to Old Wilson, and we did. I don't want this story getting around. I'd rather have his ending remain a mystery, than people thinking he went insane, and that's what they'll think, even if we show them the truth. And if we *do* show them the truth, then all hell will break loose. They'll dig up those caves, and to do that, they'll have to tear down half of downtown Portland, Morrises included. This place means a lot to a lot of people, particularly my family. There's a lot of history here."

I sat down. This was a lot to think about. Was it right to keep something this big a secret?

"But Wilson, there's a thing down there that's different from anything anyone has ever seen before. It could be proof of extraterrestrial life!"

"Look, Mel, we've been friends for a long time, but if I have to, I'll fight you. I'll deny people access, and I'll deny everything you say."

"We could be famous. Think of what this could all mean."

"The Davis' are a proud family. A great deal of that pride comes from knowing we come from a great man, a slave who freed himself and his wife, and rose to be a business owner, respected in his community. Generations of our family have looked up to his example. We are *not* going to tell people that Wilson Aaron Davis died in a stinking hole deep underground, eaten alive by alien bugs. Now, you can publish your manifest if you want, you can tell people he was shanghaied, but we are not telling the rest."

He was close to tears again. I could see how much this meant to him.

"Okay Wil, have it your way."

I agreed to his wishes, but it took me a while to get over my disappointment. Wilson had the entrance to the tunnels in his basement walled over, leaving no trace to the subterranean horrors below. We never spoke of those unbelievable events again. I put my manifest away on a shelf, and never did publicize its existence. Wilson's friendship meant too much to me. But something still bothered me. What happened to the other creatures Wilson's ancestor mentioned in his diary? What of the giant slug-things and the being he called Crazy Man? I looked around on the Internet a bit, but couldn't find what I was looking for, so I turned to my own library.

There are advantages to being a history buff, and an incorrigible book collector, and one of them is that you amass a large, specialized library of rare books. That was me. I poured over certain volumes on northwest history, particularly some old personal memoirs I had acquired at estate sales. It was tedious going, slogging through reports of fishing catches and measurements of the water level on the Willamette River, but eventually I found an interesting reference in a memoir penned by a former functionary of the Oregon Provisional Government.

"Some tales have been circulating," he wrote, "of some kind of curious beasts of decidedly unsavory nature, among children and mentally deficient derelicts who haunt public houses near the pier. No doubt stiff alcohol has affected their perceptions, and children repeat their ramblings, scaring each other."

He mentioned sightings of weird creatures six or seven times, always in the area near the Shanghai Tunnels, but dismissed them each time as the products of alcoholic imagination. And then, after the devastation of the Great Flood of 1861, when much of the city suffered the ravages of the Willamette River breaching its banks, they were never mentioned again. Could it be that simple? Alien slugs drowned in a flood? Crazy Man seemed to have disappeared without a trace, unless he was still down there. I certainly didn't want to find out.

Wilson eventually regained partial use of the three fingers on his left hand, but they remained withered and bent. His music was never the same again. He was still the best saxophone player on the West Coast, but he now played with a sadness he never had before. There was a melancholy air to every note. I wasn't the only one to notice. Melanie picked up on it right away, and brought it up to me. I had to plead ignorance.

"It's not just his music that's changed," she said to me one night. "He's a different man. We used to be close, but now the only time I feel him connect is when we're playing. I guess I should feel lucky we have that."

I took a tour of the Shanghai Tunnels a few months later. They give the public tours, along with a little lecture on the history of the tunnels, their use in kidnapping people for unwilling ship crew, and their later use as speakeasies during the Depression. I wanted to see if I could discover where Old Wilson Davis escaped from his kidnappers, but I didn't find anything. If only they knew, I couldn't help thinking, what really lies deep beneath these tunnels. There are nights I can't sleep, and I lie awake thinking about that thing down there. Whatever things you hold sacred, thank them you have no idea what's under the Shanghai Tunnels.

At the Shoe Shop of Madness

There once was a shoemaker named Schumacher. He was the worst shoemaker in the village of Knocknurn. His shoes would fall apart after only a few weeks of wear and besides that they were ugly. Because of this the shoemaker had very little business and he was going broke. One night he was sitting by himself in his workshop getting drunk and attempting to eat himself into a stupor.

He had long ago finished off a jar of plum wine and had knocked over the jar on the table. As he was about to clear the table and go to bed, he noticed there was something in the jar. He picked up the jar and to his surprise he discovered there was a naked little man inside, asleep. He grabbed the lid of the jar and screwed it on the top. He tapped the side of the jar with his finger. The little man inside did nothing so he shook the jar gently. The little man still didn't respond so he shook the jar again. This time the little man woke up. He sat

67

up and had a sick look on his face. The shoemaker couldn't believe what he saw. He shook the jar again and this time the little man threw up.

The little man in the jar looked down at himself and his eyes widened as if he were in shock. Then he looked around. He seemed surprised to discover he was sitting in a jar – a jar held by somebody much larger than himself. The little man's hands clutched at his neck. He was choking. He made a desperate gesture toward the lid and knocked on the side of the jar frantically.

Schumacher unscrewed the lid and took it off. The little man gasped and smiled weakly. He crawled over to the side of the jar and shouted at the shoemaker. "Hey, you moron! Thanks for making me puke all over myself! Where are my clothes?"

"I have no idea," Schumacher said. "I just discovered you lying in my jar, asleep."

"Oh, crap, now I remember," the little man said. "I slipped and fell into your wine jar and my clothes got soaked, so I took them off and threw them out. Then I drank all the rest of your plum wine, which was delicious. I must have passed out. Now I'm covered in my own gak. Thanks a lot."

"Who are you?" the shoemaker asked.

"I'm Artie Pinsetter, the elf. Who the Hell are you?"

"I'm Schumacher, the shoemaker."

"That figures. How about helping me get out of here?"

Suddenly realizing the import of what the little man had just told him, the shoemaker quickly screwed the lid back on the jar.

"Hey, you idiot!" the elf shouted, "I can't

breathe!"

The shoemaker picked up a nail and hammer from his workbench and clumsily punched several holes in the lid of the jar.

"There," he said. "Now you can breathe."

"Let me out of here, you asshole!"

Schumacher thought for a minute. "No, I think I'll keep you in there. If you're an elf, you're magic and you can do things for me."

The elf's face turned red and he looked very angry. He folded his arms across his chest. "I won't do it. I won't do anything for you. I'm naked and standing in a pool of my own throw-up. This doesn't exactly make me want to help you."

"You said you liked the wine? I have more. I have lots more."

Schumacher had unwittingly hit upon one of Artie Pinsetter's many weaknesses. He did like a good drink. The elf's glower softened a bit.

"What about sausages?" the little magical creature asked.

"Yes, I have sausages. You can have as much sausage and wine as you like, as long as you'll help me with some things."

The elf stroked his little beard as if he were thinking. An evil gleam came to his eyes. "Okay Schumacher, I'll help you as long as you keep the sausages and wine coming."

"And you have to promise not to escape."

"Oh, okay, I promise not to escape," the elf said, a mocking tone in his voice. "You caught me, so I have to do your bidding. Now how about letting me get cleaned up?"

Schumacher put the kettle on the stove to heat some water. When the water was warm he poured some into a cup, unscrewed the lid of the jar and slid the elf into the tiny makeshift bathtub. While Artie was having his bath, the shoemaker washed the elf's clothes in another cup and put them by the fire to dry.

After his bath, Artie Pinsetter, wrapped in a blanket Schumacher made from some rags he kept around to polish shoes, stretched out by the fire.

"More wine!" the elf demanded.

The shoemaker brought him some wine in a thimble. The elf drank it all and then shouted for more. "Just bring the bottle," he said. He smiled an evil little smile at Schumacher as if he were planning something.

After the elf had drunk so much wine he passed out, Schumacher put him back in the jar and screwed on the lid before he went upstairs to go to sleep. As he crept up the stairs, he licked his lips in anticipation, planning exactly how the elf would make him rich.

The next morning, the sound of pounding on his shop's door interrupted the shoemaker at breakfast. He quickly put the elf's jar on a shelf behind some piles of leather and opened the door. A man carrying a pair of shoes burst through the door, shouting.

"Schumacher, you're a disgrace as a shoemaker! Look at these things! You sold them to me a mere two weeks ago and already they're coming apart. Disgraceful!"

The shoemaker took the shoes from the man and looked at them. Mournfully he reached into his pocket, took out some money and paid the man back. "I'm sorry," was all he could manage.

After the man left, Schumacher went back to his

breakfast. He brought the jar over to his table and unscrewed the lid, sliding the elf onto the table.

"It's about time," Pinsetter complained. "I'm ready for breakfast too. Bring me a bottle."

"Isn't it a bit early to start drinking?"

"Did you agree to keep me supplied with plum wine and sausages or not?"

The shoemaker got up and brought over a bottle of wine for the elf.

"Here's my problem," Schumacher said. "I'm a terrible shoemaker. My shoes fall apart. I'm going broke."

The elf gulped down a thimbleful of plum wine and belched. "That's unfortunate for you. I'd say you were in the wrong profession."

"I was thinking – maybe you could make shoes for me."

"Do I look like a shoemaker to you?"

"No, of course not... but you're magic. You could use your magic to make shoes. Really good shoes. Shoes people would pay a lot of money for."

Pinsetter stroked his beard and looked around the little workshop. He smiled to himself as if he were thinking evil thoughts. Finally, he answered.

"Okay Schumacher, I'll make shoes for you. They'll be the best shoes you or anyone else has ever seen. But, I only work at night, and only in private. I don't want you finding out my secrets. Got me?"

"Oh, yes, of course! I wouldn't think of trying to discover your secrets," Schumacher lied. He very much wanted to learn the elf's secrets so that maybe he could become a great shoemaker on his own. Then again, why bother? If the elf would do all the work, why should he even try to discover his secrets? Either way, he couldn't lose!

"All right, it's settled then. Go make me some sausages."

Without a word the shoemaker scurried off to make some sausages for the elf.

That night as the shoemaker lay in his bed, trying to go to sleep, he heard all manner of strange noises coming from his workshop. There were scrapes and squeaks, hoots and howls, strange shuffling noises, the tap-tapping of a little hammer, crashes, bangs, bells, whistling, and three times the whole building shook so hard it seemed like it might come apart. The shoemaker trembled in his bed, pulling his covers up tight around his shoulders. How could making shoes cause such a ruckus? Far from thinking of spying on the elf, the shoemaker was glad he was safe in his own bed. At least he hoped he was safe.

In the morning, after a few fitful hours of sleep, Schumacher snuck down the stairs as quietly as he could. He peeked into his workshop, hoping he wouldn't see the entire room in a shambles. To his delight, everything seemed right, and there were five pairs of shoes on his worktable. His eyes wide with disbelief, he hurried to the table and picked up one of the shoes. It was exquisite! It was unlike any shoe he had ever seen before. The style was completely unique and there didn't seem to be a single seam in the entire shoe. There were no laces either. The top and sides were covered in the finest scroll-work he had ever seen on a piece of leather. The sole was thick, yet supple.

Thinking he would try on the shoe, Schumacher sat down and lifted his foot.

"No! Don't do it!" Artie shouted from the other

side of the room. "Don't put on that shoe!"

"Huh?" Schumacher grunted. "Why not?"

"It's... uh... made for – ah – one person. Yes... Each of those shoes is made for a certain person, and only they can put them on."

Schumacher put the shoe down. "Oh. I see." Considering what an amazing job the elf had done on the shoes, Schumacher figured he might as well humor him. "You only made five pair?"

"What the Hell? You ungrateful slob!" The elf picked up an empty wine bottle and threw it at the shoemaker. It hit him in the head, fell to the floor, and broke. "You want people to get suspicious? How many shoes can you make in one night? Asshole!"

The elf was right, so Schumacher didn't argue. Sheepishly he got up to fetch the broom to clean up the broken glass.

"Make me some sausages while you're up," the elf bellowed from his makeshift bed. "I have a hell of a hangover."

Later that day another irate customer stormed into Schumacher's shop. He threw a ripped and worn pair of shoes at the shoemaker.

"Schumacher, your shoes are crap! I demand my money back!"

"Wait a minute, my friend," Schumacher cajoled. "I have a brand new line of shoes. These are the best shoes ever made. Let me give you a pair for free. If you like them, send your friends here for all their footwear needs." He handed the man a pair of the elf's new shoes. "Try these on."

The man sat down and slipped the shoes on. He stood up and walked back and forth. A smile spread across his face.

"These are wonderful," he beamed with delight. "They're the most comfortable shoes I've ever worn. I'll take them." He took Schumacher's shirt collar in his fist and drew him close. "But if they fall apart like that last pair I'll be back here and do more than throw a couple of shoes at you."

"They won't fall apart, I promise," Schumacher trembled.

The man released his grip on Schumacher and left the shop, a spring in his step. From his hiding place behind a mug, the elf smiled to himself.

That night after Schumacher had given the elf another bottle of plum wine and a plate of sausages, and had promised once again not to watch the elf as he made shoes, Schumacher lay in his bed, his covers pulled up to his neck, trying to fall asleep. At the stroke of midnight, the strange noises started again. Schumacher squeezed his eyes shut and tried to pretend he didn't hear the horrible slurping sounds from his workshop. All the terrible noises from the previous evening repeated themselves; the shrieks and squeals, the cries and hoots, the tapping of the infernal little hammer, and when Schumacher had scrunched down under his covers in an effort to deny what he was hearing, the house shook again. It was as if the house itself was trembling at some abhorrent activity the shoemaker had no desire to know about. The house shook once again and then a third time, this time so hard it seemed to actually lift off of the foundation and come crashing down. Dust rained from the rafters.

When he finally drifted off to sleep, Schumacher's dreams were filled with repulsive images of the tiny elf laughing in his face and people throwing pair after pair of shoes at him.

In the morning, the shoemaker was awakened by an insistent pounding at his door. He threw on his clothes and hurried down the stairs. As he neared the door he could hear voices on the other side. "Hurry up, Schumacher!" they called. "Let us in!" When he opened the door three people rushed in.

"We want your new shoes!" one of them exclaimed.

"We saw the shoes you gave Hossenweimer," a lady said. "We want some shoes just like those. They're beautiful!"

"Hossenweimer says they're the most comfortable shoes he's ever worn, and he could walk all day without his feet growing tired," the third, an old man, added.

"Wonderful, my friends, wonderful!" Schumacher burbled, flabbergasted. "Right this way." He led them into his workshop, hoping the elf was nowhere to be seen. As the four entered the workshop they came to a sudden stop. The room was a shambles. Chairs were overturned, bits of leather were strewn about, tools were on the floor, a lamp was broken and oil had spilled onto the floor, and in one corner was a pile of a fine gray powder ash. In spite of the mess in the room, there on the worktable were ten brand new pairs of shoes, next to the four from the previous day.

"My... my apologies, friends. I've been hard at work, you see. These new shoes I make are very difficult."

The three visitors each picked a pair of shoes up from the table and examined them. They couldn't believe what they saw.

"The workmanship is impeccable," the old man

marveled. "However did you do it, Schumacher? You've never shown this kind of skill before."

"And they're so beautiful!" the woman cooed. "Look at the decorative leather work. This almost looks like a pair of eyes on this one."

"We'll each take a pair," the first man stated. "How much are they?"

Schumacher thought quickly. How much could he sell these for? "One hundred marks?" he ventured.

"One hundred marks?" the old man contested.

"You seem to like them an awful lot, Herr Dusselkringle. You'll not find shoes like this anywhere else," Schumacher said.

The three visitors grumbled, but they each paid the one hundred marks and left with smiles on their faces. As soon as they had gone the shoemaker returned to his workshop and began cleaning.

"You see? You're getting rich already," the elf declared, coming out from under the worktable. "I need more wine."

Schumacher put the broom aside and went to the pantry for a bottle of wine. He may have just made three hundred marks, but this elf's wine consumption was getting expensive.

That night went the same as the previous few. Schumacher lay trembling in his bed while his house shook as if possessed by unholy spirits. The cacophony of hideous noises grew so loud the shoemaker was afraid the neighbors would awaken. The walls shuddered with such force Schumacher was sure his humble domicile would collapse. The ceiling rattled and dust rained down everywhere. What depraved and arcane activities could possibly be taking place just below him? A putrid stench arose from the floor below that was so strong Schumacher was afraid he would retch, but eventually it faded away, and he was able to drift off to a fitful sleep while the tap-tap-tapping of a tiny hammer continued.

The next morning Schumacher trudged down the stairs to his workshop, wishing he could have had a better night's sleep, and wondering what he would find. It was worse than he imagined. Every shelf in the room had been ripped from the wall and smashed. The chairs were in pieces. Broken cups and plates littered the floor. The pile of ash in the corner was larger and spread farther. A corner of the hearth had been broken from the fireplace and lay on the floor. The edges of the worktable were singed, but there on the table were one hundred new pairs of shoes.

"Get me some fucking sausages," the elf growled, crawling out from a pile of rubble on the floor.

"What... what happened here?" Schumacher stammered.

"I made you some shoes," Artie barked. "And now I'm hungry. And thirsty."

The shoemaker sighed and turned to get the elf his sausages and wine. His brow furrowed. He wasn't sure there was any plum wine left. Schumacher lit the stove and put some sausages on to cook, then rummaged in the cupboards for more wine. All he could find was a small bottle of rye spirits he had opened years ago.

"This isn't going to go well," Schumacher thought to himself as he put the sausages on a plate and picked up the bottle of Korn. Timidly, he scuffed back into the workshop and presented the elf with his meal.

"What the fuck is this?" the elf roared. "A bottle of goddamn Korn? Who do you think you're dealing with here, some pansy-assed fairy? I'm Artie Pinsetter, the fucking magic elf! You promised me plum wine, and I want plum wine here by tonight or I'm not making any more damn shoes!" He threw the bottle against the fireplace and it broke into shards.

"Yes, yes, of course, Mr. Pinsetter, sir. I'll go get some now." Schumacher grabbed his coat and a pair of the elf's shoes. He let himself out the door, locking it behind him, and headed for Schicklegruber's Wine and Spirits.

People clogged the early morning street and several greeted Schumacher. The news of his marvelous shoes was spreading, and they all wanted to see them. A couple of people even tried to buy the pair he was carrying, but he made them promise to come by the shop later. When he got to Schicklegruber's, he pulled the door open and went inside.

A cheery voice greeted him. "Herr Schumacher, to what do I owe this pleasure?"

"Herr Schicklegruber, I trust you are well?"

"As well as anyone can be this early in the morning," the large man said.

"Yes, well put, Herr Schicklegruber. Have you any of that plum wine left?"

The shopkeeper looked through the racks. "You're lucky, Schumacher, I have five bottles left."

"Five bottles?" the shoemaker squeaked.

"It's very popular."

"I'll take them."

"And how shall you pay, Herr Schumacher? As I

remember, the last time you were here you cleaned out your purse."

With a pride he was unaccustomed to feeling the shoemaker placed the shoes he had brought with him on the counter. "You may have heard of the new shoes I've developed, Herr Schicklegruber. They are the finest shoes in the land."

The wine seller's eyes grew wide. He picked up the shoes and turned them over and over. "May I try them on?"

"Why certainly. Be my guest."

The heavy man flopped into a chair and pulled off his boots. After slipping on the new shoes a smile spread across his wide face. "These are wonderful!" he smiled. "Please, take the five bottles, and you have credit for your next visit!"

Schumacher thanked the man and left. As he headed for his own shop his mind was troubled. Five bottles! That ornery little elf would drink those in a few days. What would he do then? As he hurried through the streets, lost in thought, he nearly collided with the young woman who had visited his shop the previous day.

"Herr Schumacher!" she said. "I just want to compliment you on these incredible shoes. I haven't taken them off since I got them."

"That's very sweet, Fraulein Goosenbauer, but surely you jest."

"It's true. My feet feel so wonderful I don't want to ever take them off again. I have more energy than I've had in years and my husband says I have a new rosy glow about me. I also have a strange craving to eat jewelry."

"Well, be sure to tell all your friends where you got them. I have been very busy and I have plenty."

Schumacher excused himself and continued on his way. Before long he caught sight of the old man who had visited his shop. He was also wearing his new shoes. The old man shuffled along as if in a trance. Schumacher noticed the shoes seemed to be a darker shade than they had been the day before, a deep coppery red, and the man's skin was pale, almost ghostlike. The shoemaker approached him.

"Greetings Herr Dusselkringle! How are you enjoying your new shoes?"

The old man made no response.

Schumacher noticed the old man carried a dead cat by the tail, and when he got near a wall, his arm sprang up and slammed the cat against the wall. The man shuffled forward a few steps, slammed the cat against the wall, leaving a dark red spot, then shuffled forward once more, again smacking the poor dead animal against the wall.As Herr Dusselkringle shambled off, Schumacher noticed there was some strange wriggling worm-like thing that seemed to be growing out of his neck. Confused by the man's strange actions the shoemaker resumed the trek to his shop.

When he arrived at his shop, Schumacher could hear the elf's voice from inside. He quietly turned the key in the lock and pushed the door open a few inches. Pinsetter was inside singing some unhallowed verse.

"That is not bread which can eternal fry, and with strange onions even cooks may cry."

A sense of dread filling his soul, the shoemaker stepped into his shop, the bottles of wine clanking together as he almost dropped them. The elf's voice suddenly stopped. What could those terrible words have meant?

"Uh... hello, Mr. Pinsetter, I've brought the wine!" Schumacher attempted to sound cheery, though he felt no such emotion.

"It's about damn time!" Artie barked. He grabbed a bottle from the shoemaker and toddled off into a dark corner.

Before Schumacher could react, a voice from behind startled him.

"Where are these marvelous shoes I've been hearing so much about?"

Schumacher turned to see Klinkenstein, a farmer from the edge of town, on his doorstep. There were more people behind him. They pushed their way into the shop and looked around expectantly.

"We want to buy your new shoes we've been hearing about!" they exclaimed.

The next few days were a dream to Schumacher. More people arrived every hour to buy his shoes. Every night Schumacher would hide in his bedroom while the elf performed his accursed magic and the shoemaker would tremble in fear of his house collapsing. The shoemaker was becoming the richest man in town. He had raised the price for the bewitching shoes three times, and still no one could resist owning a pair. Schumacher was a wreck worrying about what would happen when the last of the plum wine was gone.

The second night after he visited Herr Schicklegruber's Spirit Shop, the shoemaker was once again in his bedroom waiting for the dreadful magic to begin. He was hiding under the bed because he fully expected the roof to come caving in. What would Artie Pinsetter do when he drank the last drop of the wine he demanded as payment for his services? Stop making shoes, that was for sure, but what else? What if he chose to vent his anger by destroying the shoe shop or doing something unspeakable to Schumacher himself? These thoughts were weighing heavily on the shoemaker's mind when he heard the loathsome bedlam begin in his workshop. Fear of what the future held made him take the first step in what may have been the most unfortunate series of events in his life. Schumacher edged out from under his bed and began to skulk down the stairs, wishing for all his life that he could go and hide under his bed till morning. If he could only wake up to find all traces of the elf and his monstrous bargain gone.

As he timidly set foot on each stair the dread he felt grew greater. The preternatural howling that arose from the room below curdled his imagination and he almost turned and fled back to his bedroom. Only his conviction that he had to do something or he would have no more shoes to sell kept him inching toward the workshop. A sound as loud as a clap of thunder exploded from the floor below, followed by the infernal tap-tap-tapping of that hellish hammer. When he got a whiff of a foul stench, his stomach turned over and he almost retched. Yet another step down, and he could hear Artie Pinsetter's voice, amplified by some unnatural circumstance, morbidly shrieking an arcane rhythmic chant.

"Pt'oowee m'ug-w'ump Cthulhu R'lyeh wgah'nagl fatgums... Pt'oowee m'ug-w'ump!" the blasphemous elf wailed, "Cthulhu R'lyeh wakka wakka fatgums!"

What tenebrous language was this, and what arcane import did the words have? With trepidation, he rounded the corner to his workshop, not knowing what ill-fated tableau he would find there. What he saw shook his faith in his own sanity. What he was expecting to see before him was the fiendish elf busily at work on the table, pounding and sewing together hunks of leather at breakneck speed. What he spied instead, stopped him in his tracks. He was unable to breathe, unable to even conceive what was going on in his own wretched home.

A sickly flickering lutescent glow bathed the entire room. Hideous shadows danced madly across the walls. A few dozen pairs of the shoes littered the floor, and dear gods, they were moving! Each one had four claw-like appendages that they used to pull themselves across the floor, leaving a trail of acrid ichor behind their execrable bodies. On the end of two rugose stalks were gruesome blinking eye-things, unlike any eyes the shoemaker had ever seen before, full of malevolence and... hunger. These repellent crawling shoe-things weren't the worst of what Schumacher gazed upon, however. What he saw next made his blood run cold as he fell back against the wall to steady himself.

The sickly, amber glow from the fireplace illuminated the most unimaginable spectacle possible. Even though the opening of his fireplace was well over four feet wide, as well as tall, it was completely blocked by a massive gelatinous tentacle convulsing with obscene menace. The baneful elf was next to the horrendous appendage, hammer and chisel in hand, attempting to pry one of the repugnant shoe creatures from its scaly surface. Dear gods, if that single tentacle filled the entire fireplace opening, what was on the other side?

The shoemaker managed to stumble a couple of steps into the room before his knees buckled and he fell to the floor, muttering, "What... what..."

Startled, Artie looked up from his iniquitous ritual and his eyes grew wide with rage. "*No!* You fucking moron! You're not supposed to come in here! You idiot!"

The elf threw down the hammer and chisel, and ran for Schumacher, but it was too late. Three of the crawling shoe creatures reached the shoemaker. Digging their ghastly claws into Schumacher's skin, the timorous interloper screeched in pain. As he passed into unconsciousness, Schumacher's last sight was the elf jabbing at the hideous little creatures with a fork. The shoemaker slipped into a horrifying dream whereupon he was being eaten by gigantic shoes.

***

Even before Schumacher opened his eyes, he felt something sharp poking him in the ribs. He forced his eyes open and saw Artie jabbing him with the fork.

"Wake up, you stupid fucking idiot!" the elf yelled.

"Ow! Stop poking me," the shoemaker said.

"I asked only two things of you," Pinsetter groused. "Keep me supplied with food and drink, and stay the fuck out of the workshop when I'm doing magic! How hard is that? Where's my damn wine, by the way?"

"It's all gone. The wine shop has no more." Schumacher looked around. They were in his kitchen. "How did we get in here? The last thing I remember..." and then he went silent, not wanting to remember the last thing he remembered.

"I dragged you in here. And a good thing I did, too."

"But how-"

"I'm an elf. A *magic* elf. Just because I'm small doesn't mean I'm a goddamn weakling. You've really mucked things up. You won't have many shoes to sell today because you interrupted me."

Thinking back to the unbelievable sights he had seen just a short time ago, Schumacher shuddered, but managed a question. "That thing... that degenerate aberration lurking in my fireplace..."

"Forget you ever saw that. It's beyond your comprehension anyway."

Pushed to his limit, the shoemaker managed to raise his voice. "Tell me!" he pleaded, close to toppling off the edge of his sanity.

"Oh, all right," the elf said. "You might as well know. I was so pissed off when you captured me I vowed to get back at you – teach you a lesson! I agreed to make shoes for you, but instead I was going to conjure up one of the Great Old Ones, an abhorrent creature, a terrible god-like thing that lies dead, but dreaming, to come and tear this house asunder and hopefully kill you in the process."

Schumacher could do little else but sit and listen to the abysmal tale the elf was telling, barely able to comprehend what he was hearing.

"But I fucked up," Pinsetter continued. "Look at

this piece of crap." He pulled a small pamphlet from his satchel. It was rumpled and stained, some of the writing on the cover faded by the deep red stains. In tiny crabbed handwriting, Schumacher could make out the words *The Secret Magickal Experiments of Manny the Barber of Prague.* "I spilled wine on the damn thing. Can't read half the spells anymore."

The shoemaker took the tiny book from Pinsetter and opened it, turning through the wrinkled and discolored pages. "What is this?" he asked.

Angrily, the elf grabbed the book from Schumacher. "It's a fucking book of magical spells. I won it from a drunken troll who was a terrible card player. He told me this Manny guy was the barber for some jerk named Joseph Nadeh who robbed graves and knew all kinds of magic, so the barber would write down the spells this guy bragged about when he was getting his hair cut. That's this book. As you can see, it's all screwed up now. I couldn't read the end of the ritual. Instead of conjuring up the damnable beast all I got was one tentacle! That tentacle was covered in despicable, grotesque parasites, some kind of anagogic leeches, living on the mucilaginous form of the accursed god, sucking its life-giving juices into their own confounded shells. I figured I could make the best of a bad situation and turn the little fuckers into shoes. Something bad was sure to come of that."

The shoemaker stared at the elf in disbelief.

"But the otherworldly leeches made great shoes! The best shoes anyone's ever seen! What are the odds of that?" The elf threw the book on the floor.

"Now you know the whole story. If you want me to keep making you rich, go get me more wine. If they're out of plum wine, get something else. Something good."

Schumacher just stared into space, shaking, as his mind tried to make sense of everything that had happened recently... a giant unknown god of some kind in his fireplace... shoes that were really living creatures...

"Well, get up and go, you useless piece of shit!"

The elf's harsh voice jarred him into action. He got up off the floor and with trepidation in his heart he headed for Schicklegruber's Spirits.

People filled the streets and it seemed like half of them were wearing the revolting shoe-things. Strangely, the shoes seemed to be all different shades of red or brown, regardless of what color they had originally been. Many stopped to compliment the shoemaker as they passed.

"These are the most wonderful shoes I've ever worn, Herr Schumacher! I never want to take them off!"

Schumacher trembled as he noticed that these same people seemed to have sprouted loathsome wriggling worm-like things on various parts of their bodies.

The shoemaker approached Schicklegruber's shop with a sense of foreboding. The shutters were drawn, which wasn't a good sign. Schumacher pulled the door open with a prolonged creak. The air inside was stuffy and still. It was difficult to see since the shutters blocked all but a few feeble rays of light. He stepped in and closed the door behind him. Dust was everywhere.

"Herr Schicklegruber?" the shoemaker

apprehensively called.

From behind the counter a shuffling noise startled Schumacher. "Herr Schicklegruber?" he called again.

A horrible hulk stood up behind the counter, its features a twisted travesty of a human. Schumacher recognized it as what had once been the wine shop's owner. His right arm was no longer an arm, but was an obscenely writhing sickly moss colored tendril that snaked out toward the shoemaker.

Its puffy, distended lips parted, and from deep within the gibbous shell a voice reminiscent of a cross between a frog's croak and a snake's hiss uttered, "Schhhhhhumacher... sssssssso niccccce to sssssee you..."

The shoemaker's blood ran cold and he backed away from the horrid simulacrum of a man.

"Don't go, frieeeend," the thing croaked. "Like...Schhhhhhumacher... come... ssssit..."

Schumacher edged his way into the shop's interior. "I just came for some wine," he stammered.

"Goood..." the thing slobbered, "Have credit... take wiiiine...." It shuffled forward. Its feet, encased in the execrable pulsating bodies of the shoe-things, which now ran all the way up past the man's knees, were swollen, blood red. Grotesque bulbous eyes on the ends of stalks peered about. "Shhhhoes ssssssso comfortable, Herr Schhhhhhhumacher.... I never... take offfff..."

In a panic, Schumacher grabbed the closest case of wine, hefted it onto his shoulder and ran out of the building. Back on the street, he noticed a number of the people wearing his shoes were showing signs of unusual changes. He didn't look too closely because he was afraid of what he might see. It was apparent, however, that the village of Knocknurn was undergoing an opprobrious transmogrification of some sort, and it was connected to the despicable shoe-things that duplicitous elf was conjuring. Schumacher resolved to do something about the deplorable situation.

By the time the shoemaker turned the latch on his shop door, he had decided to destroy all the unsold shoes and send the elf on his way. He set the case of wine in the kitchen. The accursed little elf was nowhere to be seen. Perhaps he had left! Schumacher almost let himself feel relieved at the thought. Back in the workshop he started gathering the shoes together. Before he could complete the task somebody pushed open his door and stepped in. It was Beckenbaumnoodle, a dairy farmer from the North edge of the village. From the corner of his eye, Schumacher could see his feet were encased in the pestiferous shoe-things, which had sprouted eyes and a mouth full of jagged teeth. Looking up at the man, he saw his face had undergone a shocking change since he had last seen him. His neck had disappeared and his head was squat, frog-like. He had thick, black lips which went from one side of his face to the other. Each of his scaly greenish hands had a grip on one of his children, who glanced about in terror.

"Herrr Schhhhhhumacccccher...." the miserably mutated man uttered in a disquieting drone, "love shooooes... sssssso comfortaaaable.... Need ssssshoessss... for cccccchildrennnn...."

The children stared at Schumacher, a look of horror in their eyes. "No we don't, sir," they pleaded, "We're fine!"

The thing that had once been Beckenbaumnoodle hoisted the children in the air so they were level with his bloated face. Its blubbery black lips parted wickedly and a dusky tongue snaked forth, playing across the children's faces, as if it was tasting them. The mouth twisted into a nauseating imitation of a smile.

"Yesssss... neeed sssshoessss... for childrennnn..."

"H-here," the shoemaker stuttered, holding out two pairs of shoes.

"You put them onnnnn..." the depraved thing ordered.

Gingerly, the shoemaker crept forward and slipped the shoes on the children, who whimpered and started to cry.

"Goood," the hulking brute drawled, "Shhhhhhoes goood..." He turned and shambled through the door, dragging the children behind him.

Schumacher kicked the door shut, gathered up all the remaining shoes, and headed for the fireplace.

"And what the fuck do you think you're doing?" a familiar voice asked. Artie Pinsetter stood before the fireplace wielding a fork as if it was a trident.

"I'm going to burn these abominations before they have a chance to harm anyone else."

"I don't think so, asshole." The elf threw the fork so hard it stuck in the shoemaker's knee.

"Son of a bitch!" Schumacher dropped the shoes.

"Now get me some of that wine I saw you bring in."

"Yes, sir." Schumacher grimaced, plucking the

fork from his knee. He limped into the kitchen and opened the wooden crate. The shoemaker pulled out a bottle and looked at it. A white wine from the Rhine. He limped back into the workshop with the bottle, hoping it would suffice, and handed it over to the elf.

"Liebfraumilch! Are you fucking kidding me?" Artie frowned. "It will have to do," he muttered and popped the cork. "Just for that, you're going to help me tonight. Maybe with you helping we can make up for the interruption last night." With that, the elf tottered off into a dark corner with his bottle.

Schumacher busied himself with cleaning up his unfortunate workshop. It had seen a considerable amount of damage the past few days. As he was cleaning, he eyed the inert bodies of the horrific shoe leeches and wondered what Eldritch magic transformed them into footwear, and what the ultimate outcome of this calamitous bargain would be. While sweeping the growing pile of ashes into a corner, he heard the sound of breaking glass from outside. Peeking through the shutters, he saw something happening at the tailor shop across the street.

For the second time that day his blood ran cold and he wondered if what his eyes beheld could possibly be true. Some sort of invidious mongrel creatures, at least a half-dozen of them, were swarming over the wall of the tailor shop. They appeared to be abominable hybrids of humanity and... something else. Instead of arms, they had squirming snake-like appendages. They had broken the window and were trying to crawl into the shop through the opening. Each one of them had on what had once been a pair of the shoemaker's wondrous new shoes, but now more closely resembled bloated giant red leeches with eyes and mouths that completely engulfed the wearer's legs up to the knees.

Suddenly the tailor burst from the door, waving a large pair of shears and attacked the impure creations on his wall, viciously stabbing them over and over. A sickly green, viscous fluid oozed from the wounds. Lethargically, the beasts turned their attention to the tailor. First their black tongues darted forth, playing across the tailor's body, and then wrapping around his head and limbs, holding him in place, while the things swarmed around him, completely engulfing him with their tentacles. In a few minutes, they wrapped themselves around the tailor, as if they had no bones in their bodies. They formed a malignant cocoon around the doomed soul as he rolled on the ground attempting to free himself. One of the awful black tongues clamped over his mouth so he could make no sound. After a time, the feculent beings separated, and the tailor was nowhere to be seen. As if with one mind, the slithering, degenerate things crawled into the tailor shop through the open door.

Backing away from the window, his face ashen, dumbstruck by what he had just witnessed, Schumacher resolved once again to do something to stem the flow of this otherworldly pestilence. But what? He was just a poor shoemaker. Well, he wasn't so poor any more. He sat down on his workbench and tried to think of some way out of this appalling situation. After a few minutes of futilely wracking his brain, his head began to hurt, and he gave up.

Drawn by a morbid curiosity, he approached the window again and peeked out. Six ghoulish things lined up in front of the tailor's shop decked out in the finest clothes from the shop, as if they were dressed for some nightmarish ball. They were all staring straight at the shoemaker. Their fancy raiment moved in odd ways, as if macabre things were moving about underneath.

Overcome with fright, Schumacher slammed the shutter closed and ran upstairs to his bedroom. He hid under the covers trying to make sense of the situation. Obviously this deceitful elf had gotten the best of him and was turning the world upside down in revenge for being captured. Schumacher had to do something to stop the seemingly inexorable transformations that were turning his hapless customers into monsters. But what? He was no hero. Set the elf free and call it quits? But there was money to be made... For hours he ran the problems over and over in his mind, but could still think of no way out. Finally, he decided he would go along with the elf for tonight, help him harvest the diabolic parasites, sell them all the next day and then make off with all the gold he'd managed to save. The more he thought about it, the more he liked this plan. He could move to Stuttgart, make wine out of topinambur, and never, ever talk to another elf.

He busied himself collecting a few clothes and other items and packing them into a valise, ready for when he could make his escape. A few minutes before midnight, he heard the despicable elf's voice calling from the stairwell.

"Let's go, asshole! Time to get to work. And

bring me a bottle of that crappy wine."

Schumacher hurried down the stairs and into the kitchen, retrieving a bottle of Liebfraumilch for Pinsetter. He was not looking forward to the next few hours. As he entered the workshop, the elf looked at him suspiciously.

"What have you been up to today, anyway? I haven't seen much of you."

"Just, uh, enjoying my new found wealth," the shoemaker mumbled.

"Do you have gloves? Thick ones?"

"Yes, I have some leather gloves I made myself."

"They'll have to do. Get them, and then stand ready. Don't make any noise and don't interrupt. When I am ready for you, follow my instructions exactly. And don't screw up!"

The shoemaker got the gloves and stood at the back of the workshop where he thought he might be able to run out if he needed to. He watched in horror as the little magical creature lit some candles by the fireplace. The elf picked up a small drum and began to beat on it in an odd syncopated rhythm as he threw his head back and chanted in a slow, ominous voice.

"Pt'oowee m'ug-w'ump Cthulhu R'lyeh wgah'nagl fatgums... Pt'oowee m'ug-w'umpCthulhu R'lyeh wakka wakka fatgums..."

He drummed faster and his voice grew louder, more frantic, as he squawked and howled the hellish phrase over and over. He hopped about in a circle from left to right, as his voice rose to a bellow.

Schumacher thought he would go mad as the demonic chant bored into his mind, and filled him with dread.

Artie writhed faster and faster in the circle, waving one hand over his head in strange ritualistic motions as he beat the drum so fast the noise almost sounded like a single ululating wail.

Without warning he stopped moving, facing the fireplace. He groped inside his satchel while beating the drum ceaselessly. He pulled forth a handful of purplish powder and threw it into the fireplace, making an arcane signal. The powder burst into flame, emitting the most noxious fumes Schumacher had ever smelled. The elf's voice rose to a paroxysm of hysterical roaring and he spat forth once again that maniacal chant.

"Ph'nglui mglw'nafh Cthulhu R'lyeh wgah'nagl fhtagn!!!"

As the last shouted syllable trailed off, an enormous thunderclap split the air, Schumacher thought his ears would burst. The house shook at its very foundation. Lightning flashed and blinded the shoemaker for a moment. When he could see again, he silently wished he couldn't. Protruding from his fireplace was a gigantic undulating tentacle, flapping about as if it was searching for some innocent soul to snatch and mangle.

"Get over here, you fucking idiot!" Pinsetter yelled.

The elf stood at the fireplace, his hammer and chisel in hand.

Trying to keep out of the reach of the wriggling monstrosity, Schumacher edged over next to the elf. For the first time, the shoemaker noticed the wrinkled, malodorous appendage was pocked with the ghastly parasites, greedily sucking ichor into their bodies.

Pinsetter peered up at Schumacher. "When I

scrape them off, you grab them and set them on the table, upside down. Be careful and don't let them grab onto you, or you'll be sorry."

The elf poked the chisel under one of things and hit the end with his hammer. The disgusting leech-like creature popped off the tentacle with a sickening mewling sound and landed on the floor, it's grotesque eyes agog. Schumacher stared at it in disgust.

"Pick it up, you moron!" Artie said.

The shoemaker gaped at the revolting abomination, his stomach turning at the thought of touching it. Hesitantly, he reached out and lifted it into the air. With reluctance, he turned the repugnant thing over. What he saw made his head swim. The bottom of the organism was covered with slimy greenish goo and protruding from its underbelly were several horrible rippling suckers, each of them quavering as if possessed with a corrupt hunger. It reached out one of its flagitious grasping claws and grabbed one of Schumacher's fingers with such force he nearly swooned. Fortunately, he was wearing a thick leather glove or his finger would have been severed.

"Dammit! I told you to be careful," the elf clamored. "Put it on the table and get back here. We have to work fast!"

Schumacher set the wriggling, sucking shoe-thing on the table, where it writhed and twisted, its tiny arms reaching toward Schumacher. The shoemaker returned to the elf's side and they continued harvesting the abominable leeches.

For several hellish hours Schumacher worked alongside the tiny thaumaturge, harvesting the parasitic atrocities. Together they collected two hundred of the despicable creatures, the elf only pausing to chug more wine. By morning they had one hundred pair of the monstrosities lined up on the table, each of them squirming on their backs, their suckers opening and closing hungrily. Their pitiful mewling noises drove Schumacher to the brink of madness.

Artie hopped on the table and pulled a tiny bottle from his satchel. He pulled out the cork and poured some of its grainy contents into his hand. He then sprinkled the grains on one of the caterwauling sanguisuges. In a few seconds it stopped moving. Before Schumacher's eyes it transformed into a beautiful shoe etched with delicate scroll-work.

"Hey, good for nothing piece of shit!" Pinsetter snapped. "Go get me another bottle."

On his way to the kitchen Schumacher snuck upstairs, got his valise, and stowed it in the kitchen. He wanted to be ready to make his escape. Grabbing two bottles of wine, he headed back to the workshop. Pinsetter was just finishing his iniquitous alchemy on the last of the contemptible leeches. There were now one hundred pair of beautiful shoes lined up on the table, just waiting for the shoemaker to sell them.

Schumacher gave one bottle of the wine to the elf and pulled the cork from the other. He could use a drink himself. Fortified with half a bottle of Liebfraumilch in his belly Schumacher threw open the front door to wait for the crowds to come demanding his marvelous shoes. When the door swung inward a crowd of people tumbled in, falling on the floor. At least some of them were people. Some of them were wearing clothes, like people, but there was something desperately wrong with their bodies.

One of them had what looked like a lobster claw for a hand. Another had no head, just two stalks protruding from its neck, with bulbous eyes on the end of the stalks. Still, another had no legs, just a row of foul tentacles on the bottom of its torso, twisting like a dying snakes. Each of the distressingly deformed beasts held onto one or two normal people, all of which trembled in despair. One of the mongrel things spoke.

"Herrrr Schuuuumaccccher... we neeed sssssshoessss.... for friendssssss..."

One of the unfortunate prisoners managed to find his voice. "Herr Schumacher, we're fine, really. We don't need new shoes. Our shoes have plenty of wear in them yet. Really!"

"I sssssaid you need sssssssshoessss..."the mongrel thing hissed, and it reached down to its prisoner's feet and tore off his shoes with a long reptilian tongue, taking two toes in the process. The prisoner squirmed and howled in pain.

"Will you ssssssell ussssss sssssshoesssss... Herrrrr Schuuuuuuumacccccher?"

"Why- why, of course, sir. Just one hundred marks a pair. A special today," Schumacher sputtered.

"We pay you.... tomorrrrrowwww..."

The things dragged their captives to the workshop, fitted them with shoes, and then dragged them back out in the street, but not before the talkative one bade the shoemaker goodbye.

"Thank you, Herrrr Schuuuumaccccccher... sssssoon everyone will have your sssssplendid sssshoessss... everyone...."

This wasn't going very well for Schumacher. If they didn't pay for the shoes, how would he have the money to start a new life somewhere far away? While these thoughts were tumbling around in his mind, the shoemaker looked out of the door.

The street was in chaos. All around people were being accosted by harrowingly malformed beasts, and the beasts all wore what once had been Schumacher's marvelous shoes.

"Hey! There he is!" somebody shouted, and for the first time the shoemaker noticed a small crowd of normal people in front of his shop. They carried a motley array of implements with them-pitchforks, sickles, large knives. A few of them even had guns. One of them heaved a huge stone at Schumacher. It hit him square on the forehead. The shoemaker backed inside his shop and locked the door. He heard one of them shout, "let's get him!" And then there was a terrible pounding at his door.

Schumacher ran to a window and peered through the shutter. The damned monstrosities were molesting a company of musicians. One ill-fated atrocity which no longer had a head or arms, but only snake-like appendages where they used to be, was thrusting the extremity that took the place of its head in and out of the bell of a horn. The creature shivered with unholy pleasure. Another thing which was nothing more than a blob wearing a dress seized a small harp and caressed the strings while it attempted to engulf the instrument with its body. Across the street, the tailor shop was completely covered in frightful transmutated beings, each of them pulling, pushing and pounding on the building, which shook until it finally collapsed in a heap of rubble. Having reduced the shop to debris, the horde of nightmare things turned their attention to the crowd of people who were still pounding on Schumacher's door.

The mass of undulating, reptilian flesh oozed across the street and set upon the congregation at the shoemaker's door. Schumacher thought he would go insane as their piercing cries tore his soul in two. The door burst open, the hapless humans and the forsaken freaks all spilled into the shop. Schumacher shrank back in terror and despair. The mass of oozing, undulating plasm things spread across the bodies of the humans who attempted to gain their freedom by attacking the mucilaginous mass with their pitchforks and sickles.

One of the morbid monstrosities broke away from the grappling horde and stood up. Its torso was twisted at a grotesque angle and its skin was covered in globose welts that throbbed as if they were alive. What had once been a pair of the bedeviled shoes where now swollen red appendages where its legs had been.

"Weee neeed sssssshoessss," it wheezed, "Everyone musssst know... joy... of Sssssschumaccccher's sssshoessss..."

The shoemaker fought the urge to vomit and managed to whimper, "Of... of course... just one hundred marks a pair..."

The thing lurched toward the workshop. "Neeed sssssshoessss... now.... Everyone musssst be happy..."

Scooping up the shoe-things from the table, it skittered back to the struggling group and began slipping shoes onto the feet of the normal people.

In a few moments the doomed mob lay on the floor, silent, as if in a trance. The afflicted beasts gathered up the people and left.

Schumacher glanced around at the deplorable state of his hopeless habiliment. Odorous muck festered in putrid pools everywhere he looked. This hadn't gone as he planned at all. All the shoes were gone and he had gotten no money for them. How was he ever going to put this calamitous episode behind him and start a new life? How could he abandon his dream of being a rich man? Deciding it couldn't be helped and that his most propitious course of action was to make a getaway, fast, he stole into the kitchen and retrieved his valise. Looking around, he couldn't see Pinsetter anywhere so he headed for the front door.

He discovered the front door now closed and the malicious little elf standing in front of it.

"Just where the fuck do you think you're going?" Artie asked.

The shoemaker could find no words to offer as an excuse. "Thought you could escape my revenge, didn't you? I don't think so!" The elf erupted into a torrent of maniacal laughter that chilled the shoemaker's blood down to his soul. "This village is going to be remembered for your miserly mistake. Cthulhu's parasites are growing tired of the anemic blood of humans. They want their original host, and the power its fluids provide. They're tearing this pathetic little hamlet apart, and soon That Which Is Not Dead will rise. It will wipe this crappy little town from the face of the Earth! But, it won't fucking stop there! Knocknurn will be only a harbinger of what is to come. Before long, even death may die!" Once again the elf erupted in a diabolic and hysterical laughter.

Seeing no other hope, Schumacher resolved he had to get away, and even though he was weak with terror, he started to crawl toward the stairs.

"You're not going anywhere, you pathetic idiot!" the elf cried. He made a mysterious gesture and the shoemaker found himself pinned to the floor, unable to move. "You brought this fate upon this miserable berg, and there's no fucking way you're going to avoid what's coming to you." With a smirk on his face Artie strolled into the workshop and came back with a pair of the execrable shoes. "That's right – I saved a pair for you. The very last pair!"

Schumacher finally found his voice, though feeble. "Please... no... no..."

The elf burst into laughter once again, as he slipped the shoe-things onto Schumacher's feet. At once the shoemaker felt a wave of exhilaration come over him, followed by a wave of tiny, painful pinpricks all over his feet. "For the love of God!" he wailed. "Please stop it! Not me! I gave you... everything you asked for!"

"I'll never forgive you for the Liebfraumilch, you asshole! Eat shit!"

As Schumacher slipped into a coma of terror, thunderous crashes boomed. His poor shop was wracked with calamitous shocks. The elf's shrill chortling filled his consciousness, until it was all too much and he was consumed by madness...

ETERNAL BEAUTY
(inspired by HPL's Ex Oblivione)

It **was fifty years ago** I first looked upon
Eternal Beauty, and I think of that day with
both happiness and regret. I had just come from
an appointment in an unfamiliar part of town and
was searching for a bus stop when I saw that
infernal flower peeking through a gap in a
curtained window.

The house was drab and shabby, like the
surrounding neighborhood. White paint was
peeling from the walls; the steps to the front door
were worn. In sharp contrast, encased in a delicate
vase just inside the front window, stood a rose
blossom of a most singular configuration, its
blinding white petals gleaming in the sunlight.

Though I worked at a menial office job my
passion was that of growing things, and I had a
particular passion for roses. I had read so many

books and magazines on the subject, and poured over every gardening catalog endlessly that I considered myself a bit of an expert. Even from a distance I could tell I had never seen a rose like this. I found myself creeping closer to the house, straining to get a better look at the bloom. Its white petals virtually glowed, shining like a beacon from the dirty window sill.

Standing close to the window, peering at the bloom, entranced, I was lost to the world around me. That flower had me in its spell already. I had never seen anything so beautiful. It called to me, and I wanted nothing more than to touch it. My hand rose toward the vase without any conscious thought on my part. At that instant the curtain fluttered and the glorious plant was snatched away. I looked up to see a wrinkled face glowering at me, its features twisted with what could only be described as a mixture of fear and hate. The window came crashing down and the curtains snapped shut.

I was shocked back to reality. Here I was standing outside a stranger's house, peeking in a window. What was I thinking?Clearly whomever that face belonged to resented the invasion of privacy... but that rose. I had to get a better look at it. I was familiar with every variety available in this country, and this one wasn't any of those. Was this some startling new hybrid that hadn't been released to the public yet? I had to find out. Knocking timidly at the worn door, I hoped against hope that whomever was inside would be willing to let me see the elegant prize. I really don't like intruding on strangers, but the perfection of those white petals sang such a beautiful song. I had to see it again.

No one answered, so I knocked again, louder. Still no answer.

"Hello?" I called. "I'm sorry to disturb you, but I saw your rose in the window. It's so beautiful. I'd just like a chance to get a better look." And after another moment of silence, "I grow roses myself."

I knocked again. "Hello?"

Propriety was getting the best of me, and crestfallen, I was about to leave when I heard the lock turn and the door opened a few inches. An ancient, weary eye peered at me from inside.

"You hear it, don't you?" a shaky voice asked.

"Excuse me?"

"The rose. It calls to you. I can tell."

"Well, yes. I've never seen another one like it. I'd love to get a closer look."

He stared up at me, his ancient eyes narrow with suspicion, but I also thought I saw something else there. Pity. And now that I think back on it, a bit of deviousness.

After a few moments I heard the lock turn and he pulled the door open. I thought he was going to let me in, but he blocked the entrance and pointed at me.

"You have to promise me one thing."

"Yes, of course," I replied.

"You can't touch it."

The request seemed a little paranoid, but I was desperate to see the flower, so I agreed. He shuffled to the side and I stepped into his house. I looked around the room and it was pretty much as I expected. A couch and overstuffed chairs several decades out of date and dilapidated. A heavy dining room table of dark wood peeked from the next room. Cobwebs clogged the corners.

What surprised me was how barren the place was. By all appearances he had lived here for many years, but there was nothing to indicate that. There were no knickknacks, no memorabilia, nothing to reflect the man's personality or interests; no books, magazines or newspapers, not even a TV. There was nothing but furniture, and a single clear glass vase that held the white rose.

He ushered me over to a small table and I gazed down at the stunning bloom. It was even more breathtaking than I had first thought. The petals were perfectly symmetrical, perfectly formed. Each row was of uniform measure, and now that I had a chance to gaze at it in all its glory I could see a small splotch of the deepest red on one of the inner petals. Rather than spoiling the effect, this one blemish, so like a single drop of blood surrounded by the angelic white, only intensified the beauty. The subtle perfume, intoxicating. The total effect was hypnotic. More than hypnotic; it was as if I was staring at the essence of life, the endless wonder of the universe encapsulated in this one perfect flower. I wanted nothing more than to stare at the rose for the rest of my days.

"How old would you say that flower is?" the old man asked, jolting me out of my trance.

There were no signs of wilt on the bloom at all. "Obviously it's been cut recently," I said. "No more than a few hours ago."

"That flower has been in my possession forty-seven years and twenty-two days," he said.

"Please," I said, the scorn evident in my voice.

He simply opened a drawer in the table and removed a stack of photographs, throwing them on the table.

"Take a look," he said.

I picked up the pictures and rifled through the stack. Some were obviously quite old, their edges worn, their colors fading, others were black and white, with crinkled edges of the type I'd seen in my grandparent's albums. Each held a picture of a rose, a white rose; and when I examined them closely, they all appeared to be the same bloom. The size was the same, the color looked right, and the perfect placement of the petals mirrored the flower in the vase in front of me. And that tiny red drop on the inner petal- it was there, in every photo. I looked in disbelief from flower to photo, and back again, trying to find some minute difference, but there was none. It appeared that every flower in the photographs was the very same bloom in the vase before me.

"It's a clone or something," I said.

"No clone could be *that* perfect of a copy" he replied. "That white rose is not only beauty, not only perfection, it's eternity as well."

I reached toward the vase to get a closer look, but he slapped my hand back with more strength than I thought he could possess.

"I told you. No touching."

I clasped my hands behind my back and bent to get a better look. The longer I gazed, the more beautiful it became. The scent was mesmerizing. I felt as if I could spend the rest of my life staring at its perfection.

A sharp pain in my shoulder interrupted my reverie. The old man's bony hand dug into my shoulder blade. He was pinching me. I shook my head. I didn't realize I had been that lost in my thoughts.

"It cast its spell on you," he said.

I took a deep breath and stood up.

"I guess it did. What variety is it?"

"I call it Eternal Beauty, but you won't find it listed anywhere. That's the only one in existence."

He must have seen the look of disbelief on my face because he continued.

"Come, sit with me. I haven't had a guest in some time."

He led me to the dusty dining room table and we sat in rickety chairs. A plate with a cheese sandwich cut into fourths rested on the table, the only other thing I'd seen in the house besides the rose, that was of an impermanent nature.

"I was just about to eat. Have one," he said. "I insist. Eat while I tell you the story."

I picked up a section of the sandwich and took a bite, all the while watching the old coot. He settled back in the chair and smiled as he stared into the distance.

"I found the rose one night in a dream. I was young then, and full of stupidity and hope. My life was good. Money, friends, love, a good job. I had everything. Everything except peace of mind. There always seemed to be something missing, something intangible, something I couldn't even articulate, something more that I wanted. I wasn't satisfied. I couldn't be happy, knowing that thing, whatever it was, was missing from my life.

"In the daytime my mind was troubled, but every night I dreamt I was in a beautiful land, a land of purple twilights and golden valleys, shadowy groves filled with vine choked trees. I was at peace there. I felt complete. My soul lost its feeling of yearning. Wandering through this land was nothing but joy.

"Little by little I lost interest in worldly sensations. By comparison, this waking existence was pale, uninspiring. I let friendships wither, merely walking through my daily life, biding my time until I could dream once again. Each night as I passed into unconsciousness a smile came to my lips.

"I spent my nights exploring every inch of this beautiful dream land. The landscape was an ever widening panorama of natural beauty, but I never once saw another living creature. I was alone in my happiness, but that didn't concern me. It was enough to be allowed access to this heavenly dream.

"One night in a glade by an overgrown gate I came upon something surprising- a leather bound book with no title. I took the book to the base of an exquisite tree and opened it. What could this singular volume possibly contain? The pages were filled with ornate hand written script, obviously produced by several different hands.

"The tales within, by the descriptions they contained, all took place in this very land. They were stories of love and purpose, great deeds done by great people. They called the land Zakarion. The prose itself was powerful, sweeping, told with unparalleled beauty. I could barely put the book down, reading each new adventure with anticipation.

"Each morning I would wake up full of images from the stories I read in my dreams, and as I stumbled through my days the stories faded from my memory, driving me to utmost frustration. I could barely wait till the night came so I could dream once again, and read more of fabled Zakarion. What had happened to the people in these tales? Where had the inhabitants of Zakarion gone? There were no clues in the book. The answer to this question haunted me both awake and in my dreams.

"One night the story I read was about an unbelievably beautiful white rose that cast a spell on everyone who beheld it. Generations of families plotted and schemed to possess the most beautiful object in the land. In the end they all destroyed one another in their jealousy and lust. As I read, I realized the places described in the fateful tale were ... familiar.

"Barely daring to hope, I looked up and gazed at the scene before me. My heart pounded ferociously. The glade before me matched exactly the scene in the book. I rose shakily to my feet and brushed some vines out of my way, and there it was. The white rose. Eternal beauty itself. I couldn't help myself. I reached out and plucked the flower from its stem, and as I did so, a thorn poked my thumb, drawing blood.

"The pain from that puncture woke me from my dream. It was just barely dawn and a faint light shown through the window, allowing me a clear view of the object in my hand. I beheld the white rose, a few drops of blood still wet on my hand. I stared at the flower, unbelieving, barely able to draw a breath. Sitting up, I touched the delicate petals tenderly. Raising the bloom to my nose I inhaled the intoxicating perfume, the scent thrilling.

"Standing, I carried the miraculous rose to the

kitchen, placing it in a short glass with some water. Surely I had to still be dreaming. I pounded my fist on the counter. The pain seemed real. Somehow my act of plucking the rose had transported it from the world of my dreams to the real world. I brought the glass to the kitchen table and sat staring at what could not possibly be.

"That was the last time I got to visit the peaceful land of my dreams. I could never again find the land of Zakarion. No matter how long or how well I slept, my nights were devoid of any kind of dreams. The images of that peaceful land faded away, as did the magnificent tales of that magical book. Try as I may, I could remember no details – only that there had been a land of supreme beauty, and I had spent years of dreams there. But, I had the rose; one exquisite, perfect reminder of that marvelous land."

The old man sat silent for a minute, a faraway look in his eyes. Then he reached, lifted his right arm with his left hand, and set the arm on the table. I realized at that moment that he had never used his right arm. His right hand was enclosed in a white glove.

"The act of plucking that rose had one other effect," he said.

He removed the white glove, revealing a shriveled, discolored hand.

"There was something in that rose, some chemical, some poison. At first there was just a loss of sensation in my thumb, where the thorn punctured my skin. Eventually, the entire thumb shriveled up and became useless. I spent thousands on medical tests, but they could never discover what was causing the atrophy. It kept spreading, slowly, year after year, until the hand became useless. The doctors recommended amputation, but I wouldn't hear of it.

"Finally my entire right arm hung useless, but at least I still had the rose. Remarkably, the rose lived on, vibrant, alive, just as my arm died. I came to learn it needed no sustenance, that it would never fade. I showed it. Entered it in competitions- and it won! It was apparent to anyone who looked upon the flower that it was the most beautiful object in the world. But when I came back to the same shows with the same rose, there began to be questions. No one would believe it was the same flower, even though they could see for themselves it was. Did the photographs lie? Did their eyes? People started saying it was some kind of fraud. Screw them. I never showed the rose again. Nobody believed me. I kept the photos though, hoping that one day someone might listen.

"The rose, the most beautiful object in the world, became the focal point of my life. I maintained a semblance of a normal life, a job that met my physical needs, only so that I could care for the wonderful flower, and spend every free moment in its presence, adoring it. I celebrated the day of my retirement for one reason- I would never again have to leave the dear beauty. Forty-seven years, twenty-two days that has been my life, and I have only one regret- the loss of Zakarion. The rose is a jealous lover. She didn't want to share me with anything, not even a dream. She weaves a tight spell. I am content to bask in her beauty, but I do miss the dreams."

The old man fixed his gaze on me.

"What say you? The ramblings of a demented

old man?"

I returned his gaze. Even though I wasn't looking at it, I could feel the presence of that beautiful object, could feel it calling to me.

"I believe every word," I said.

He smiled, but I thought I could see sadness in his eyes. Rising, he went into the kitchen and returned with paper and pen.

"Write down your name and address," he said. "I may want to get in touch with you again."

I gladly complied. Anything to keep the lines of communication open, so that perhaps I could catch another glimpse of the beautiful white rose. He drew the vase close and stared intently at the flower. I thanked him for letting me see the fabulous treasure and telling me his story, and then I let myself out.

Over the next few days I could think of nothing else but that rose. My dearest love, my Christina, called and wanted to do something, but I was too distracted, and declined. How could I explain what had happened, what thoughts filled my mind? The old man's story haunted me. Could it possibly be true? There were the photographs. I have to admit I was trying to think of some excuse to go see the old codger, just to get another glimpse of that supreme beauty. I was having difficulty thinking of anything else. On the third day I got a letter from him.

"Come see me," he wrote. "I have something for you. Let yourself in."

There was a key taped to the letter. He must have sent it the same day we met. Without hesitation I went straight to his house, not daring to imagine what he wanted. I knocked on the door, but there was no answer, so I let myself in.

"Hello?" I called. "I got your letter." There was no answer. "Hello?"

He wasn't in the living room, dining room or kitchen

"Hello?"

A sense of unease rising, I stepped into the dusty hallway and stepped cautiously toward the door at the end.

"Are you here?"

A lump in my throat, I turned the knob on the door to what must be his bedroom, and timidly pushed the door open.

"Hello? I got your letter."

Sun shone through a window, bathing everything in a languid glow. My breath quickened when I spotted the rose in its vase on the nightstand, and there in the bed was the old man. I thought at first that he was sleeping, but after standing there frozen for a few moments, watching him, there was little doubt. He wasn't breathing.

My eyes went back to the nightstand and spotted a small pill bottle. Quickly crossing the space, I picked up the bottle. Prescription sleeping pills, and the bottle was empty. I looked over at the man who seemed to be resting so peacefully. He was holding a piece of paper. Ever so gently I eased the paper from his fingers and read what was written.

"Take her. She's yours now. Care for her. Guard her jealously. I know you feel her spell. I've gone to try and find my dream land. Will this take me there? I have no idea. Perhaps not. Who knows what happens when we leave? Perhaps there is nothing out there. The regret of having lost that peaceful land grows too strong. Having found somebody who will care for the rose, I've made up my mind. Even if I don't find my way back to Zakarion, I'll be free of the Eternal Beauty."

My eyes went to the rose. There seemed to be a change. Where was that one blood red splotch of color I remembered with such detail? I folded the paper, put it in my pocket, and reached toward the vase holding my breath, excitement coursing through my body. I would at last be allowed to touch the delicate flower. Ever so tenderly my fingers closed around the stem, and as they did so, I felt a sharp prick. A thorn had caught me. As I drew my hand back a single drop of blood dripped from the wound and fell upon one of the inner petals. What had I done? I'd defiled the most beautiful object I'd ever seen, but when I picked up the vase, I could see the new blemish intensified the beauty, just as the old one had. Peering at the bloom intently I thought, "It's mine. I own the most perfect, the most beautiful thing in the world."

As I left the room I looked back at the withered body in the bed.

"Poor soul," I thought. "What a wasted life."

I clutched the vase tightly, my thumb stinging where the thorn had punctured it, and left the dusty shell of a house, feeling a mixture of emotions. Pity for the old man, excitement for my own future, hope, and amazement at my good fortune. I possessed Eternal Beauty. What more could anyone want?

THE THING THAT CAME TO HAUNT ADAMSKI

The two young women looked down at the shards of plastic on the floor. "Eww," said Claire, her nose wrinkling in disgust at an odor only she could smell. "That's gross!"

"You think that's bad, you should taste what I'm tasting," Klara added, her mouth grimacing in disgust. Claire and Klara were twins, and they had special powers. Claire was clairalient. Her nose was psychic. She could smell odors of things that weren't present, but had some kind of connection to what was happening around her. Klara, she was clairgustant. Her mouth was psychic. Impressions of things around her would come through her sense of taste.

"What is it you taste?" Claire asked.

"I'm not sure. I've never tasted anything like it before. It's awful, though."

116

"Same here. This thing I smell – I have no reference for it. Strange."

Just then they heard a pounding behind them, and a muffled voice. They turned and surveyed the room, but couldn't see what was making the noise. Of course Milton's apartment was always a mess, so it was hard to tell. The pounding continued, the muffled voice sounding more insistent. The twins followed the sound into the dining room where they spotted a large trunk on top of Milton's cable spool table. The pounding came from the trunk.

The two women rushed over and examined the trunk, looking for a lock. They found the latches and undid them, heaving open the lid. Gasping for air and staring up at them was Milton, his beefy body stuffed into the trunk, like a self-inflating raft that you could never get back into the package. The twins couldn't believe he fit in there. Everyone called him Milton the Monster because he was huge and resembled the cartoon character from the sixties.

A wild look in his eyes, Milton tried to pull himself from the trunk, but he was stuck. "I'll kill him!" he yelled, once he caught his breath. The women each took an arm and pulled, but they couldn't get him out. "I'll kill him!" Milton bellowed again.

"How did you get in there?" Klara asked.

Ignoring her, Milton ordered, "Get me out of here!"

With much pulling and pushing the three of them managed to get the trunk upended on the table. Milton wiggled frantically, trying to free himself. Finally, he fell off the table and landed on the floor, the trunk on top of him. There was a

117

loud thunk as he hit the floor. He got up on all fours looking like a gigantic turtle. The twins grabbed the trunk and yanked it off, ending up on the floor themselves.

Milton stood up, the crazy look still in his eyes, and spotted his keys. Grabbing them, he ran out the door, bellowing once more, "I'll kill him!"

Afraid of being left out of the action, the twins ran after him, jumping in the back seat of his rusty old Mustang just as he threw it in gear and sped away.

"Dude, who put you in the trunk?" Claire insisted, her nose wrinkling again. That awful odor had returned. She looked at her sister, who was in obvious distress, her tongue moving around inside her mouth like she had just swallowed something rancid. The twins had once briefly considered becoming a super team and fighting crime, but they gave up on the idea when they realized remote smelling and tasting were the worst super powers ever.

"I wish I could figure out what this smell is," Claire whispered to her sister.

"I know what you mean," Klara whispered back, "Even when I'm not familiar with a taste, I usually know what it is when I get a psychic tasting. This one is totally foreign. And it's really icky."

The car careened around a corner and the twins yelped in dismay.

"Take it easy, Milton!" Claire said. "Where are we going, anyway?" As if in answer to her question, the tires squealed as Milton turned the car into a driveway and pulled to a stop. Without a word Milton threw his door open and strode up to the front door of the house.

"Oh, shit," Klara said, "this is Adamski's house."

Milton pounded on the front door and yelled, "Let me in, Adamski, you jerk!"

As the twins cautiously approached the door they couldn't help noticing Adamski wasn't answering. That didn't seem to matter to Milton, since as soon as the women reached the door it gave way under Milton's pounding. The big man rushed through the doorway, his eyes searching for Adamski. As soon as the twins entered they were overcome. Claire clamped her hand over her nose and sank to the floor. Whatever produced the odor she had been smelling was in here, and the smell was overwhelming.

Klara stepped over the threshold and immediately vomited. The taste in her mouth was so repugnant she couldn't hold it in any longer. Taking no notice of the twins' distress, Milton spotted Adamski. His back was to the door, and he was sitting at a worktable cluttered with debris. The small, balding man puttered with something. In two giant steps Milton was behind him. He grabbed hold of Adamski's lab coat and lifted the man clear out of the chair.

"Why the Hell did you lock me in that trunk, Adamski?" Milton demanded. He turned the man around so they were face to face, intending to give Adamski a good smack right upside his head, but when he saw Adamski's face all he could do was utter a quiet "What the?"

The twins crept forward so they could see what had caused such a reaction. Something was wrong with Adamski's face alright. His eyes bugged out, bloodshot and distended. The skin on the left side of his face was mottled, brown and cracking. Two translucent, nubbly, waxy little fangs poked out from his mouth.

"Let me down, you muscle bound moron!" Adamski squeaked. Without a thought Milton released his grip and Adamski fell to the floor. One of the bloodshot eyeballs popped off his face and went flying. It landed near Claire, who picked it up.

"It's fake," she said, after examining it. "It's a prop!"

"What are you up to, Adamski?" Milton said.

"Give it back!" Adamski said. He scrambled across the floor, grabbed the fake eyeball and tried to stick it back on his face.

Milton turned to look at the table. It was littered with a bewildering array of seemingly incongruous materials: an open box of ping pong balls, a bag of flour, a block of paraffin, pipe cleaners, food coloring, small bottles of paint, something labeled nose putty, a myriad of books and magazines. Milton spied something and laughed. He grabbed a magazine from the table and confronted Adamski. "This is mine!" On the cover was a garish photo of a monstrous creature and the magazine bore the title "Dick Smith's Do It Yourself Monster Make-Up Handbook."

"I needed it!" Adamski said, "Really I did! Had to try and scare... it! I knew you'd never let me borrow the book, so I had to steal it."

The twins gave each other a knowing look. The scenario was becoming clear. Adamski had done this to Milton before. The trunk used to belong to Houdini, and Milton loved to show it off. All Adamski had to do was get Milton talking about the trunk, showing off the trick apparatus, and with a swift push at the right moment, Milton would fall into the trunk, trapped. It never failed. Probably one of the reasons Milton was so angry was he realized he had fallen for the old trick again.

Something troubled Klara. "What do you mean you had to scare *it*?"

Adamski's exposed eye widened in terror, and then narrowed suspiciously as he positioned himself behind Milton, peering around him at a spot beyond the table.

"It's here," Adamski trembled. "After all these years, *it's* here."

"Oh, no! Don't start with all that BS," Milton moaned. Adamski was widely regarded as a crackpot. He had published an almost endless collection of books on his alleged contacts with UFOs and aliens. Of course his books had all been debunked. Adamski was a sloppy writer, and often made claims that were easily disproved, like the time he was supposed to be in a high level meeting aboard a flying saucer, but had been seen by scores of people in Vegas gambling and flashing wads of cash.

Adamski, of course claimed this, and other such incidents, were a giant conspiracy to discredit him, but still, he had zero credibility. That didn't stop him. He continued cranking out new stories of his adventures with aliens from various planets year after year, insisting every word was true. "You've got to do better than that if you think I'm not going to beat the hell out of you for stuffing me in that trunk again."

Adamski's one unobscured eye grew even wider

and he pursed his lips. "It's really here. There's a Venusian in this room right now, and it's haunting me."

"Where is it?" Milton growled.

"Over there, in the wastebasket."

Claire padded over to the small metal mesh basket overflowing with garbage and bent down to get a good look. Perched on top of a wadded up piece of paper was what appeared to be some kind of insect, about two inches long. It waved a couple of antennae at her. She pinched her nose closed with her fingers. "Eck. It stinks! Don't you smell that?"

"I don't smell nothing," Milton said.

Klara joined her sister at the waste basket and made a retching noise. Luckily her stomach was already empty, so she couldn't vomit again. The twins looked at each other. "No wonder we couldn't figure out what it was we were tasting and smelling," Klara said to Claire. "It's an alien. It doesn't smell or taste like anything on Earth."

"Give me break," Milton said. "Adamski sees a bug in his trash and we're supposed to believe it's from Venus?"

Claire stood up. "I think he's right. Nothing on Earth smells like this."

"See? I told you!" Adamski said. "This thing flew in the window this morning, landed on my monitor and introduced itself. Apparently the inhabitants of Venus are quite different from the visions I've had all these years and they're very upset at the misinformation I've been publishing."

"Adamski, you're even more off your nut than you were before – or this thing is a fake," Milton said. He stomped over to the waste basket and made a grab for the insectoid figure. A loud buzzing filled the air, wings popped up on the alien's back, and it flew into the air, darting straight at Milton's face. "Ow!" the big man howled, swiping at the bug thing. His cheek was bleeding. "Alright, now I am going to pulverize you, Adamski!"

"No! I didn't make it! It's real!"

"I think you should believe him," Klara said. "You know our extrasensory powers are never wrong, and they're telling us that thing is not from the Earth."

"It's from Venus, and it said it's going to haunt me for my lies. That's why I wanted to scare it. Maybe then it would go away."

"Look – I think it's dancing," Claire said, still pinching her nose closed.

The bug-like thing had landed on a blackened banana peel in the waste basket. It bobbed up and down while running in a circle and waving its antennae.

"That suits me fine," Milton said. "You and that thing can keep each other company till the end of time. I'm taking my magazine and leaving."

"No! You have to help me!" Adamski wailed. "That thing is terrible! It puts horrible images in my head. It will drive me crazy!"

"Short trip," Milton said, as his face went blank. He dropped the magazine and grabbed the edge of the table, his hand covering his eyes. The Venusian buzzed again.

"I think that's a ritual dance," Adamski said. "It did that just before it showed me its nightmare visions."

Milton wavered on his feet and the twins moved

to the side. They didn't want to be in the way if he fell over. After a minute he regained his equilibrium. He took his hand away from his eyes. All the color had drained from his face.

Klara put her hand on his shoulder and looked in his eyes. "What did you see?"

"God, it was awful," he mumbled. "There were...hordes of those bug-things swarming over unknown planets, devouring everything in sight... eating people alive... their screams, heart wrenching... each world they visited left barren, all life consumed. They're like space locusts; eating every planet in their path." The four humans turned to face the bug on the banana peel. "Is that why you're here?" Milton asked. "Is Earth going to be your next meal?"

The Venusian hummed again and the four people heard its voice in their minds. "It depends – we like Earth. Earth is funny. We don't want to kill it but we don't like that one either. He spreads lies about us. Makes us sound like weaklings. We are not weaklings. We are powerful. If that one does not change his lies, we will eat Earth."

The twins and Milton looked at Adamski, who was teetering on the verge of tears.

Claire bent down to talk to the alien creature. "What if Adamski could fix the damage he's done?" The bug hummed. "what if you dictated some new books to him? He could tell the truth about you, make the Earth quake in fear of your terrible power."

"You'd be willing to do that, wouldn't you?" Klara asked the balding man.

"Of course!" Adamski said. "Anything, anything at all!"

The Venusian bug hummed happily. It seemed to approve of the plan. Milton picked up his magazine. "I'm glad that worked out," he said.

Claire frowned again. "Something's still not right. I still smell that terrible odor. If everything is fixed, it should go away."

"You're right, sis," Klara said, "It's always worked that way before."

"There's only one thing it could be. When we first got to Milton's place we saw some broken bits of plastic on the floor. That's when we first had our extrasensory impressions."

Adamski looked at the floor, sheepishly. "After I locked Milton in the trunk I was in a hurry to find the make-up book. I knocked a Pez dispenser on the floor and stepped on it."

Milton clenched his fists. The twins could tell he was about to explode. "Which one?" he asked.

"It was Goofy."

"My 1965 Goofy Pez dispenser?"

"He'll pay for it," Klara urged.

"Forty bucks!" Milton said.

"Forty bucks?" Adamski protested.

"Pay him!" Klara said.

Adamski took out his wallet and grudgingly handed Milton two twenty-dollar bills. "Highway robbery," he said.

Claire took her fingers away from her nose, drew in a deep breath and smiled. "The smell is gone! Everything is fixed!" The Venusian buzzed. "I think you'd better get busy with your new friend," she said to Adamski.

"Right you are!" he smiled, sitting down at his computer.

As the twins and Milton left the house, Adamski

was cheerfully clacking away on his computer, the Venusian bug thing perched on the top of his head, buzzing.

***

And that's how Adamski came to actually save humankind.

KONG-TIKI

Everyone knew about the old Star Shine Club. It had once been the most elegant dining and dancing establishment in the heart of Los Angeles. A mob family owned it, and one night a rival mob family tried to move in. A dozen people died that night, and the place was shut down. Later it became a warehouse.

Those who believed in such things said it was haunted by the ghosts of those who died that night. Things disappeared, strange sounds were heard, people saw figures moving, the whole bit. I didn't know anything about that. I was here because the place was reopening tomorrow and I was the band leader.

As I strode through the front door entering the chaos of construction, I spotted Gus right away. Except for his attire, he looked exactly as he had when I knew him in the army- a short stocky man with a buzz cut and a Cuban cigar that he was never seen without. Right now he was barking orders to a dozen people simultaneously. Same old Gus Garrison. One time I had seen him and his crew erect an air strip, command post and barracks for thirty in twenty-four hours.

It didn't take him long to notice me and wave me over.

"Marcus Lameroux," he beamed as he crushed my hand and pumped it. "Are you and the boys ready for tomorrow?"

"We're ready," I replied. "But will this place be ready? Looks like there's a long way to go."

Gus frowned, stuck the cigar in his mouth and chewed on it. He looked as if he was trying to decide if he should throw me out or not.

"Marcus, you should know better than that. Have I ever failed to hit a deadline? Tomorrow, the third of October, 1959, the biggest, most astounding Tiki club on the West Coast will open for business."

"If anybody can do it, you can, Gus."

"Just look around you," Gus said, putting his arm around my shoulders and waving with the cigar.

I had to admit the transformation was astonishing. I'd seen pictures of the place during its heyday in the thirties. It was all gold and white glitz, opulent Hollywood elegance. That had all been replaced by a decor fashioned of bamboo, teak wood, hemp rope, and dried grass. Tiki statues ten feet tall by the dozens. Murals of island life and volcanoes covered the walls.

"Ain't it somethin'?" Gus beamed.

"It's something," I agreed.

A shapely young blonde woman sashayed up to Gus's side.

"Gus, darling," she cajoled, "The grass skirts are just nowhere to be seen."

"Good afternoon, Gloria," I interjected.

"Oh, hi, Mr. Lameroux. Are you in on this shindig too?"

"Musical director. I don't think I've seen you since we worked on that musical at Republic."

"That's right. *Babes in the Big House*. I guess I'll be dancin' for ya again. Me and some other girls are gonna dance the hula. Only the grass skirts keep disappearing." She shot an annoyed look at Gus.

"Can you and the girls look for them?" Gus pleaded. "I've got a million things to do."

"We *have* been, Mr. Garrison, but they just ain't anywhere." She leaned in closer. "I think something's going on, if you know what I mean."

"What *do* you mean?" I asked.

"You know, something funny. One minute they're there, then the next, they're not."

Gus was turning red.

"Gloria, I'm sure there's a reasonable explanation. You may have noticed it's a bit chaotic in here."

"Oh sure, there's an explanation, alright. Something that ain't here is takin' 'em, and then somethin' that ain't there is puttin' 'em back again. I have a feeling for stuff like this, and it don't feel right here."

Gus looked about ready to explode.

"I don't want to hear anything about ghosts, or spooks, or whatever!" he bellowed. "This club is opening tomorrow night, no matter what.

129

Everyone is going to be here! There will be no ghosts! Do you understand, Gloria?"

"Yes, Mr. Garrison."

"Now, go check again, and if you can't find them, order some more from the prop house."

"Yes, Mr. Garrison." She hurried away.

Gus glared at me, the cigar in the corner of his mouth, puffing away.

"*You* don't believe in this ghostly hogwash, do you Marcus?"

"Of course not, Gus, but we could sneak the *Moonlight Sonata* in somewhere, if you want."

At this, Gus *did* scream. People said that whenever the gangster's ghosts were around, you could hear Beethoven's *Moonlight Sonata* floating on the air.

Gus stuck the cigar between his fingers and poked at me as he shouted, "I absolutely *forbid* you to *ever* play that song on this premises. Got that, Mr. Lameroux?"

"Okay Gus," I said, backing away. "Take it easy. I was just joking."

"Well, this ain't no joke. Keep this under your hat."

He grabbed a rolled up poster from a table and laid it flat, looking back at me. The picture was of a beautiful dark skinned woman wearing a shimmering blue and green dress. Brightly colored feathers ringed her shoulders.

"Yma Sumac?"

"Right here. Tomorrow night."

"What the hell? Why haven't you publicized this, Gus? It would be the talk of the town!"

"Don't need to," he smiled. "This opening is already the talk of the town. Everybody who's anybody is going to be here. Imagine the moment when the music stops, a spot goes on, and out walks Yma Sumac. Nobody knew. The crowd will go nuts. And for weeks afterwards what will people be saying? You shoulda been there. You shoulda been at KONG-Tiki. Before long the entire city will be saying they were there, whether they were or not."

"Gus, you're a genius."

"Don't you ever forget it," he said, rolling up the poster. "You can't tell nobody."

"I need to tell the boys. We need to work up a few numbers for her."

"Okay, but they're all sworn to secrecy."

"I'm speechless. The Peruvian Princess, her first Los Angeles performance, and I'm going to play for her."

"You can thank me later," he said. "Look at what else I've got in store. This is the big payoff."

"Something bigger than Yma Sumac?"

"Take a look."

He led me to a cage of iron bars in the middle of the dance floor, standing ten feet tall and five-foot-square.

"What's this for?" I asked.

"That would be for me," a muffled voice said from behind me.

I turned and nearly fell over. I was looking straight at a seven-foot-tall lime green gorilla with red glowing eyes. I took a step back, ready to run. Gus pulled the cigar from his mouth and burst into laughter.

"Marcus Lameroux, meet KONG-Tiki!"

The gorilla stuck out his hand and, my mouth wide open, I shook it. The simian reached up and with a few twists, removed his head.

"Rico!" I exclaimed. "Gus, you don't skimp on anything."

Rico was the number one gorilla man in Hollywood.

"Do you realize what this guy is charging me?" Gus asked.

"Well, I had to dye one of my suits green," Rico said. "That wasn't cheap."

"Tomorrow Rico will hang out in the cage," Gus explained. "Rattle the bars, grab the ladies, dance around a bit. At midnight we're gonna let the mighty KONG-Tiki out of his cage and one lucky lady will win a dance with the savage beast!"

"I've been practicing waltzing wearing this thing," Rico said.

"Just one problem," I said. "You know there are no gorillas in the Caribbean?"

"What?" Gus shouted. "Ain't you never seen *King Kong*?"

"Gus, *King Kong* takes place in Africa."

Again I saw that look that meant Gus Garrison was trying to decide whether to rip me limb from limb or just throw me out.

"Well, this ain't *King Kong*," he yelled. "This is KONG-Tiki and he lives on an island in the South Pacific. Are you satisfied?"

I put my hands up.

"You're the boss, Gus."

Gloria came rushing across the dance floor. She planted herself in front of Gus, her hands on her shapely hips.

"Boss, you gotta do something about those goons in the suits. They're scarin' the girls."

Garrison visibly restrained himself before

replying.

"Gloria, dear, what are you talking about?"

"Them guys keep peekin' in the dressing room and the girls don't like it."

"What guys?"

"Them tough lookin' guys wearin' the black suits."

"Gloria, everyone around here is very busy. There's a lot to get done before tomorrow. Nobody's wearing suits today."

The young lady's brow furrowed and her jaw set.

"Gus Garrison, are you sayin' we ain't seein' what we're seein'? 'Cuz those guys are there and they're creepy."

Rico stepped forward and smiled at Gloria.

"Mr. Garrison, why don't you let me look into this?" he asked.

"Rico! I didn't know you was in on this," Gloria said. Her gorgeous face had turned a bright shade of red.

"Fine. Rico, you see what's going on."

Rico put out his furry green arm and Gloria wrapped her arms around it. They left gazing into each other's eyes. Obviously the two had some history between them.

"Those girls are gonna add a lot of atmosphere tomorrow," Gus said, "but they're almost more trouble than they're worth. Almost."

He smiled as he watched Gloria disappear backstage. Without a pause, there was a commotion at the front door. An army of workers poured through the entrance, carrying an immense object hidden beneath a tarp. Following them was a delicately featured, bronze skinned gentleman. I recognized him immediately, and was once again impressed by the amount Garrison was spending for this opening. It was Maleko Meli, the most famous sculptor in Hawaii.

"Right this way!" Gus called, directing them to an area next to the bandstand.

Garrison shook Meli's hand enthusiastically as the movers did their best to upend the object beneath the tarp. This had to be something spectacular. I made my way to the group just as the movers were pulling the tarp away.

Again my mouth dropped in astonishment. It stood twenty-five feet tall, dark and menacing. Gus was beaming from ear to ear.

"It's the biggest Tiki statue in the United States," he crowed. "Carved by the greatest artist in Hawaii!"

"Not just a Tiki statue," the artist quietly added. "This is a depiction of Tu-ka-nguha, the fierce fighter. His spirit resides in the wood and will protect this establishment."

Gazing at the statue's fearsome countenance and the ornate twelve-foot blade it held, I did not doubt the artist's word.

"I must perform the consecration ritual," Maleko said.

Gus stared down at the man before him. He got a worried look on his face.

"You ain't gotta sacrifice nothin', do ya?"

The artist closed his eyes and took a deep breath before replying.

"No, Mr. Garrison, I need only to say some prayers."

"Oh, well, that's fine then. Go ahead."

Gus dismissed the movers and wandered off to yell at somebody. I hovered near the bandstand

and watched as the artist took some kind of plants from a cloth satchel, placed them in a shallow tray at the base of the statue, and lit them. The odor wafting my way seemed familiar, like something I'd smelled when I was stationed in Hawaii.

"Marcus Lameroux, I heard I was going to be working with you."

I found myself facing a bespectacled gentleman with a quizzical grin that twisted his face into a bemused countenance. He held out his hand and I shook it.

"Melvin Silverman," he said.

"The man of a million sounds!" I smiled.

"None other," he replied. "Gus hired me to lend jungle ambiance to your music. Bird calls, monkey sounds, a few lion roars, things like that."

"Even Martin Denny couldn't ask for more," I quipped. "Gus is really going all out for this party."

"Indeed," Melvin said. "Talk of this opening is all over town. Anyone who's anyone will be here tomorrow night."

I glanced past Melvin at the sculptor kneeling before the gigantic Tiki statue. On the far side of the statue, out of his sight, leaned a bulky man wearing a black pin-striped suit twenty years out of date. He looked like the man who had been bothering Gloria, so I thought I would see what was up. I shook Silverman's hand again.

"Mel," I said, "This is going to be a gas. I'll see you tomorrow."

I headed toward the sculpture but the strange man was gone. I had only taken my eyes off of him for a second. He couldn't have gotten far. I looked around, but he was nowhere to be seen.

Finding Gus, I excused myself. It was going to be a busy night. The boys and I had to work up some numbers for Miss Sumac. They were going to be excited to be playing for a real life princess. As I left the building I was nervous. Something wasn't right. That disappearing goon bothered me, as did the complaints of the dancers.

***

The next day I arrived at the club two hours before show time, nervous but excited. Most of the boys were already there, tuning up. As per Gus's instructions, formal attire had been banned. We were all wearing khaki slacks and garish Hawaiian shirts.

The boys were joking about the marquee above the bandstand- Marcus and the Royal Tiki Orchestra. I had to admit it had a ring to it. Silverman was there, testing his mic, a glass of water with a lemon wedge in hand. I nodded to him as I unpacked my guitar.

Taking a moment to look around I was astounded by the progress made since I left. Gus and his crew must have worked all night. I had to admit the place looked spectacular. Lighted torches lent an exotic ambiance to the space. Teak wood and bamboo glowed in the flickering torchlight. The tables and booths ringing the dance floor were each guarded by their own little Tiki statue. Six bartenders mixed rum cocktails behind a bar decorated with carved coconut shells.

A nervous buzz filled the air. The hula dancers, looking gorgeous in their grass skirts, practiced their moves one last time. Rico was in his cage, red eyes glowing, shaking his bars and whistling at the girls.

If Gus was nervous, he didn't show it. Looking like he was on vacation, his outlandish shirt putting everyone else's to shame, he smiled at one and all, making rounds, wishing everyone good luck. He was a different man from the bellowing behemoth we had seen yesterday. Sauntering toward me, cigar between his fingers, huge grin on his face, he shook my hand warmly.

"You like the sign?" he asked.

"I like the name. We may keep it."

A crash came from the bar. An entire tray of drinks lay smashed on the floor. As Gus went to investigate I swear I saw a man wearing a black pinstripe suit fading into the background. In the next hour several other odd mishaps took place. A fire in the storeroom left a slight burnt smell in the air. One of the stage lights blew up, and the crew scrambled to readjust the lighting plan. A couple of the guest tables just fell over, with nobody even near them. Some of the decorative masks on the wall fell down, for no apparent reason. Little things. Things that taken by themselves really meant nothing. You'd expect there to be last minute mishaps, but still, it seemed strange.

I wasn't the only one seeing guys wearing black suits. Seemed like everyone was catching glimpses of strange men wearing dark suits. They were there for a second and then they were gone. I could tell the girls were spooked, and they weren't the only ones. Still, what can you do about something you *think* you saw? I chalked it up to opening night jitters.

Finally, a few minutes to eight, all the little crises dealt with, Gus, still looking cool, stepped up to the mic.

"Attention everyone! Places, please! Ready at the bar? Rico, this is it! Ladies, let's shake them hips! Maestro? Music, please!"

Nodding to Gus, I gave the boys a downbeat and we launched into "Quiet Village". Spread across the room, the girls waved their arms and undulated in the best Hollywood imitation of a hula dance. Rico, inside his cage, rattled the bars for effect. Silverman started in with the bird calls and Gus raised his hands.

"Let them in!" he ordered.

The doors were thrown wide and in they came, the best Los Angeles had to offer. Leading the charge was none other than Hedda Hopper, one of her spectacular hats, rimmed with peacock feathers, bobbing as she led the parade. The Bogarts were there. Maila Nurmi slunk in, underneath dark glasses and a big floppy hat. Busby Berkeley was seen, as was Lena Horne, seemingly every Los Angeles society columnist, young hopefuls and high rollers alike. Just like Silverman had said, anyone who was anyone was there.

Gus's crew, well-rehearsed, made sure they all got the royal treatment. Leis were thrown around every neck, drinks came fast, and every table had their very own hula dancer. Rico, in his green gorilla suit thumped his chest and grunted every time anyone passed close. Even the most jaded socialites found themselves gazing in amazement at the decor. Gus's exuberant extravagance had paid off. Five minutes after the doors opened and the place was a hit. All he had to do was keep it up for another six hours.

I led the boys seamlessly into "Taboo," accompanied by Silverman's frog croaks, and watched as a few couples made their way to the dance floor. Glancing around the room, my smile faded. I swear I saw those goons in the black suits lurking in the shadows. I put them out of my mind and set about paying attention to the task at hand- providing the best musical entertainment for this opening. A good show tonight could mean a steady gig for months. The boys could use the money.

By the looks and sounds of things we were doing our job well. I had never heard Bartella coax such sweet sounds from his vibes, and the rhythm section was right on the money. The hula girls were charming the crowd, and Rico in his cage was the center of attention. The more adventurous ladies would walk just a little too close to his cage and he would make a grab. He always just missed, of course, and the ladies would run screaming into their escorts' arms.

As I led the band into the opening bars of "Caravan," I had to admit that Gus had really pulled it off. I could barely wait for Yma Sumac's entrance. It would be the perfect capper for a spectacular evening. Silverman left his mic and sidled up next to me.

"Marcus, do you notice anything strange about the gorilla?" he whispered.

I turned my attention to the cage, trying to ignore a strange figure in a black suit I thought I caught a glimpse of.

"Not really, Mel."

139

"Did he seem that tall to you before?"

I looked again. Rico's head nearly brushed the top of the cage.

"You know, I think you're right. Yesterday when I met Rico he stood about seven feet tall."

"I figure that cage is about ten feet tall."

"And Rico looks about nine and a half."

"Yah. But how could that be?"

I peered hard at the cage. There was no doubt about it. Rico looked taller. He slammed against the bars and I swear the entire cage nearly collapsed. I scanned the room to see if Gus was around. He was making the rounds, schmoozing it up. I thought about getting his attention, but what could I tell him – Garrison, the green gorilla seems to have grown a couple of feet?

My attention back on the cage, it was clear something weird was going on. The gorilla now more than filled the cage. He couldn't even stand up straight, he was so tall. Rico let out a howl that sent chills down my spine. That didn't sound like an actor. That was the sound of a wild beast. He flexed his massive arms and stood up to his full height, ripping the cage from the floor. The dancers nearest the cage all ran back, gasping in surprise, staring at the sight of a twelve-foot-tall green gorilla hoisting a ten-foot metal cage in the air.

There was no denying it. That gorilla was growing. Or Rico was growing. Or they both were. There wasn't time to figure it out because now the gorilla had lifted the cage over its head and thrown it into the crowd. Everyone was able to get out of the way except one guy who was drunk and couldn't run fast enough. The cage landed smack dab on top of him. Was this some act Gus and Rico had worked up? Most of the crowd seemed to think so, as there was applause and nervous laughter.

Rico beat his chest triumphantly and gave another savage cry. He was really playing his part. Gus ran across the room and grabbed the gorilla's enormous arm, attempting to pull him to the side. Rico just raised the arm, lifting Gus into the air, grabbed him around the waist, and threw him aside. Garrison, not a small man, sailed through the air, landed on a table and fell to the floor. I had a sneaking suspicion this wasn't an act.

That giant ape raised its hands, bellowed, and I swear he grew three more feet. By now the room was silent. All my musicians had stopped playing and were staring at the emerald beast. The dancing had stopped. Nobody was talking. Everyone was waiting to see what would happen next, and what happened next was Gus ran across the room and grabbed one of the torches.

Backed by a half dozen strong men, he advanced on the giant ape, waving the torch. The beast's glowing red eyes glowered at them and it gestured angrily. Rico was a good actor, but I swear this seemed more like a wild creature than a man in a suit. Besides, the thing now stood a full twenty feet tall. Gus was a brave man. He'd proven that in the war, but I didn't think he ever anticipated battling a giant green gorilla, surrounded by a room full of innocent bystanders. He stepped right up to the beast and shoved the fire as close to its face as he could get.

The ape batted the torch away and grunted at his attackers. At Gus's signal they all threw themselves at the thing, wrapping themselves around its legs and arms. The gorilla staggered, momentarily confused. I looked up at those inhuman glowing eyes, and by all that's holy, I thought I saw one of those goons in the black suits perched on its shoulder. In just a few short minutes this opening had gone from a scene of gaiety and amusement to one of insanity.

The creature ripped Gus from its right arm and threw him across the room. It plucked another man from its left arm and flipped him in the air with a grunt. Reaching down, the ape grabbed two more men from its legs, smashed them together and dropped them to the floor. They didn't get up. Ignoring the last two men still clinging to its waist, the gorilla cast its gaze around the room, and finding what it was looking for, loped across the dance floor, men and women alike scurrying out of the way.

The thing was fast and had no trouble capturing its prize. In one swift motion it scooped up Gloria, who screamed in panic and beat against its giant furry hand. KONG-Tiki raised the girl to his face and grunted. Gloria took one look at those evil red eyes and fainted.

Amidst this impossible scene a sound caught my attention. A torturous loud creak came from the far end of the bandstand, like the sound of a hundred-foot wooden door squeaking on hinges long ago gone rusty. When I saw what made that sound, that's when things got truly bizarre. I was no longer sure I was in charge of my senses as I saw that giant tiki statue come to life and stand up on its stubby little wooden legs. My own legs got shaky and I sat down fast as I watched the statue thrust its blade in the air and lurch across the floor toward the big green ape.

My brain did a quick inventory of what it knew to be true. I was the band leader at the grand opening of the country's biggest tiki bar, and a twenty-five-foot-tall tiki statue had just come to life and was about to battle a giant green gorilla. That's what my eyes were telling me, but my brain was having a hard time accepting it. I watched, dumbfounded, as the ambulatory wooden sculpture lumbered toward the ape. KONG-Tiki had spotted the statue, and the ape's red eyes glowed even brighter. The effigy was taller, but the ape more than made up for it in bulk.

Tu-ka-nguha stomped its feet and the whole building shook It swung its blade in a wide arc, and incredibly, drew blood. A trickle of red liquid appeared on the ape's chest. The beast's eyes glowed so bright they lit up the scene, and it roared with rage. The tiki god wasted no time. Swinging its spear again, it sliced across the ape's stomach, drawing more blood. Surprised, the green gorilla dropped Gloria, raised its arms high and launched itself at the statue, an ear splitting roar escaping from its lungs.

The tiki statue rocked but didn't fall. At such close quarters its blade was of little use, so it tried to wrap its wooden arms around the beast. The gorilla simply lifted the statue in the air and sent it crashing to the floor. That's when two of those black suited spooks appeared above the wooden god, and somehow they lifted it back to a standing position. In the name of sanity, I needed to know I wasn't out of my head hallucinating, so I looked over at Silverman. He must have been wondering the same thing, because he was looking at me, his mouth wide open.

A deafening crash drew our attention. KONG-Tiki had smashed a table over the statue's head, and now they were both pummeling each other with their fists, each blow sending shock waves through the air. The statue leaned forward and rammed its head into the ape's stomach, sending the gorilla flying through the air, landing on top of the bar, demolishing it. If they kept this up, they'd bring the entire building down.

The crowd ran for the doors, only to find them blocked by rough looking goons wearing black pin-striped suits and carrying wicked looking guns. As frightened as they were of the giant creatures, nobody wanted to go up against the sure fire threat of gangsters toting gats, so the mob milled aimlessly, trying to stay away from the toughs and out of the destructive path of the warring giants.

***

The gorilla found Gloria, still passed out, and hoisted her onto its shoulder. The moving wooden statue, its spear pointed at the ape's chest, lumbered forward. A few brave souls had grabbed torches and surrounded the duo. KONG-Tiki roared savagely and snatched a table, using it as a shield. The gorilla rushed the statue, knocking it over. It then jumped on top of the effigy and started beating it with the table.

That's when the lights went out. For a second the only illumination came from the torches, casting an eerie flickering glimmer on the battle. After a few short seconds a spotlight flashed on, throwing its glare on a lone figure on the stage. Bless him, a single duty bound lighting technician had remained at his post, and on cue he had done his job. Caught in the brilliance of the spot was a commanding figure- a statuesque woman adorned from neck to floor in a skin tight blue and green sequined dress. Her flawless bronze skin was radiant, and her dark eyes flashed with passion. An elaborate headdress fashioned of feathers and jewels accentuated the woman's royal bearing.

It was Yma Sumac, the Peruvian princess, and all eyes were riveted on her. One arm rose and she turned toward me. Our eyes locked as she made a simple downward motion with her outstretched hand. I knew exactly what she meant. Rising, I stage whispered to the boys.

"Yma's vamp number two. And play it sweet."

The boys picked up the cue flawlessly and we laid down a musical bed for the princess. She raised her arms regally, took a deep breath, and when she sang, magic happened. Yma Sumac didn't sing regular songs with words, her voice was like a force of nature. She sang sounds, and this night she reached deep inside the Earth and pulled forth a volcano of sound. It was like the primal gods and goddesses of the jungle were singing through her. Yma's voice rumbled and bubbled, and when she sang she was a goddess that demanded obedience. Everyone who heard her stopped, mesmerized. She wove a magical spell, as the sound bubbled up from some deep well inside her, pouring forth, hypnotizing everyone in the building. Her music tore through the air, leaving us all helpless in her spell. With just pure passionate sound, she calmed everyone's souls. I

Lee Widener

felt it myself. You couldn't resist her. A sense of peace embraced the crowd. They stopped screaming, and the aimless running subsided.

They say that music soothes the savage beast, and dear God, that's exactly what happened. Yma's voice grew in power and beauty as the lilting notes filled the air. The giant ape stopped cold and stood up, dropping the table. It grunted and stared at the vision of beauty in the spotlight. She held her arms out toward the beast and improvised a melody meant solely for its ears. KONG-Tiki stepped off the wooden statue and swayed a bit. I don't know if it was reacting to the music or was just unsteady on its feet, but it rocked back and forth a few times, before falling backward. A couple of guys caught Gloria before she hit the ground, and a good thing too, or she would have been crushed beneath the weight of that hairy monster.

KONG-Tiki went down with a crash, and then, right in front of everyone's eyes, it shrank. In a few seconds it was just seven feet tall again. Gus stepped forward and ripped off the mask. There lay Rico, out cold. The tiki statue had also stopped moving. It was, once again, just a carved piece of wood. That wasn't the end of our problems, though. Those spooky looking toughs with the tommy guns were floating through the crowd, and from the sounds people made when they touched by the ghosts, it wasn't a very pleasant feeling. They screamed, and some fell to the ground, quivering in pain.

I had an idea, and even though Gus had expressly forbidden me to play this song, I had to give it a try.

"Okay boys," I announced. "Beethoven time."

146

We had worked up a version of the *Moonlight Sonata*, just because I thought it might come in handy. Most people knew about the legend surrounding this building; the gangster massacre, the ghosts, and how people kept hearing Beethoven's melancholy melody.

Bartella on the vibes and Maselli on flute quietly opened the number, while I chimed in on guitar, and Miss Sumac, bless her heart, joined in from the stage. The somber tones filled the air, and unbelievably, it had an effect. All the ghosts, at once, floated up toward the ceiling, and they didn't look as solid as they had before.

I don't know why this was working, other than maybe Yma Sumac, the Peruvian princess, really was some kind of musical magician. Maybe her voice had some kind of mystical power. We continued to play while Yma sang Beethoven's melody loud and clear, and right before our eyes, the ghosts faded into nothingness.

***

The club had to be closed for a week to make repairs, but everything turned out better than could have been expected. Nobody had been seriously injured, and Gus claimed everything had been staged. KONG-Tiki was an instant legend. Reviewers raved about the opening night. When everything was rebuilt and the club reopened, without the cage and green gorilla, the club was filled to the brim. Gus hired us for a six-month run. Yma Sumac was an even bigger legend than she had been before. For those of us who knew the truth, she had saved our lives.

147

The tiki statue never moved again, but guests at the club loved having their pictures taken with it, and a legend grew up around the figure that it was lucky to kiss the thing. I'm not sure if that's true, but I know for a fact it once came to life to fight a giant green gorilla. I know. I was there.

SLEEPER UNDER THE SEA

"**Someone in this room** is very sad," Madame Narrova intoned, bowing her head.

Her accent sounded East European. I couldn't place the country exactly. Me and the boys were set to go on after Madame finished her act. She was the latest big thing as far as stage psychics went. I hadn't caught sight of her yet, but I pictured a dark haired, olive skinned matron in a long gypsy dress and shawl, clutching a crystal ball. Her voice came from the other side of the curtains.

"I hear the name Beatrice. Beatrice wants to talk to someone here. She speaks to me from the other side. She says... She says she's come for Christine. Does that mean anything to anyone?"

The crowd, of course, was enraptured. I could tell; you could've heard a pin drop in that room. Someone was crying.

"You, ma'am," Madame Narrova called. "Are

149

you Christine?"

Quietly, from the audience, a woman's voice.

"Beatrice was my sister. She passed away six months ago."

"She says Fluffy is fine. He's there with her and they're both at peace."

The woman in the audience sobbed.

"Fluffy was my precious little puppy. They were both killed in a terrible auto accident."

From around the room, hushed whispers.

"She's good," I whispered to Mel Silverman, waiting next to me.

"She's a fake," he said. "Even the bit about Fluffy. The whole thing was in the papers."

"Remember, everyone," Madame Narrova said, her voice deep. "The veil between this world and the next is but a fog that can be pierced by the light of a pure heart. Keep your hearts pure and live every moment as if it were important, because it is."

She must have bowed because the crowd applauded. That was our cue. The curtains parted, and our bandstand, pushed by six strong stagehands, rolled forward. I quietly counted us down and we launched into our signature number, Quiet Village. Mel went right into his bird calls.

As the band swung into action I took a quick peek over my shoulder at Madame Narrova, who was being ushered off-stage by a burly bodyguard and my heart almost skipped a beat. Boy had I been wrong! She looked more like a Hollywood model than an old gypsy lady. As she disappeared around the corner I turned my attention back to the band. It was our opening night and I didn't want to screw up.

For this gig me and the boys were known as Marcus Lameroux and His Hawaiian-aires. We'd just spent six months playing at KONG-Tiki on the mainland, so when this offer to play at a fancy resort in Hilo, Hawaii, came up I figured the boys deserved a nice tropical vacation. Since we'd be playing a mixture of Exotica and Hawaiian music, I brought Mel Silverman along. He was still the best sound effects guy on the West Coast.

During our gig at KONG-Tiki we had honed our sound to perfection. We didn't have any horns at all, keeping the vibes, guitar and flute forward, and our percussion section tight. We were always willing to try out something different, and recently one of the boys brought back this crazy thing called a didgeridoo from Australia. It wasn't exactly Hawaiian, but most in the audience were tourists, and they just wanted to hear something exotic. That didgeridoo fit the bill nicely. It sounded something like a lion snoring.

We neared the end of our first number, and that's when we pulled out all the stops. The percussionists launched into their jungle beat, loud and wild, while a line of hula girls sashayed onto the stage. The audience applauded appreciatively. This is what they came for- a little taste of the islands, even if it wasn't exactly authentic. While the hula dancers wiggled their hips, our secret weapon stepped forward and took her place at the mic. Maia was a local girl whose voice could entrance even the most hard-hearted seafaring gob. We'd hired her to do ooo-aaa-ooo type vocals over the top of our melodies, and also sing a few songs in Hawaiian. The crowds ate that kind of stuff up.

By the looks of the smiles on the rube's faces I

could tell we'd hit our mark, and I relaxed. By the time Maselli started blowing his didgeridoo for the big finale' we had them in the palm of our hands. The rest of the set went flawlessly, and as we took our bows, the crowd let us know they liked what they'd heard. May twenty-second, 1960 would go down in my book as a great opening night. Most of the boys headed for the bar or the beach, but I'd seen a face in the audience that had my head ticking.

There he was, a nattily attired gray haired old gent, sitting by himself at a front table, writing in a notebook and sipping a drink. I ambled up to the table and stuck out my hand.

"Professor Kelley, I've always wanted to meet you."

He looked up from the notebook and smiled, grasping my hand firmly.

"Why thank you, maestro, that's a great compliment coming from the talented Marcus Lameroux. Won't you join me?"

"Please, I'm no maestro," I said, sitting at the table. "I've been a fan of your writing for years. Loved that piece on Easter Island you did for National Geographic."

He smiled even wider and winked.

"And that article was the tip of the iceberg. There was so much I couldn't tell."

I was about to ask what he meant by that when a short, rotund man with slicked back hair bustled up to the table. Oh brother. It was Sy Greenberg, New York transplant to Hilo, and the owner of the Hilo Luxury Resort. My boss. He had relocated to the islands on the advice of a doctor, to calm his nerves. It didn't work.

"Sorry to interrupt, Professor," he said, not even looking at the man. "Lameroux, that was disgusting tonight, a total disappointment."

I took a deep breath.

"The crowd seemed to enjoy it," I said.

"The crowd? What do they know? Bunch of rubes. Punch it up for tomorrow's show, or we'll be having a serious conversation."

"Excuse me, Mr. Greenberg," the Professor interjected. "I quite enjoyed the show."

"Yes, well, fine." Greenberg shot me an evil look before he bustled off to make somebody else's night miserable.

"Are you here for business or pleasure, Professor?"

"A little bit of both. I'm investigating Madame Narrova."

"That psychic lady? Isn't that a bit out of your line?"

"Not at all. Archaeology and cultural history are not my only fields. I research and write in many fields. Archaeology, anthropology, parapsychology, it's all connected. Are you familiar with the name Elizabeth Drewsy?"

It's a good thing I wasn't drinking because I would have choked.

"Are you telling me you're Elizabeth Drewsy? That hack in Fate magazine?"

"I am Elizabeth Drewsy, and I stand by every word I've ever written in that name."

This was a hard pill to swallow. The professor had a handful of academic degrees and was highly respected.

"No offense, professor, I just never associated you with all that mumbo jumbo claptrap. You're

153

doing some kind of an expose' on Narrova? I hear she's a fake."

"Not at all. Believe me, she's quite genuine. I've witnessed many incredible occurrences involving her powers."

"Powers? Really?"

"There was a family in New Haven. The great-grandfather had died, leaving a fortune to the most destitute branch of the family. Only he forgot to tell anyone where he'd hidden it. Narrova contacted him, and the family is now quite comfortable with their inheritance. Located several lost children. Made contact with a dead scientist and correctly transcribed missing fragments of an unfinished formula that is to this very day used to manufacture a new synthetic compound. Not only could she have not known the formula- nobody on the planet except the dead scientist could have. Would you like to see for yourself? She's holding a séance tonight and you're welcome to attend as my guest, if you're interested."

He didn't have to ask me twice. Whether this Madame Narrova was a charlatan or not, attending a séance with the esteemed Professor Kelley was an opportunity of a lifetime. It would be entertaining, no matter what happened. Besides, after what happened at KONG-Tiki, I'd learned there are things in this world that just can't be explained.

"I'd be delighted, Professor."

"Fine, then," he said, standing and gathering his papers. "The séance is at midnight. Meet me in the lobby a little before."

"I'll be there."

To be honest I was glad for this distraction. I'm a city boy. I love the night life, the hub-bub, the parties. The boys were having a great time on this island gig, hanging out on the beach, learning to surf, chasing after local girls, but I was bored stiff. Here in Hilo *we* were the only nightlife- besides the endless luaus for the tourists. How many roast pigs can you eat? And don't get me started on poi.

I killed time waiting for the festivities in the bar listening to the radio and devouring a copy of the LA Times that had just arrived that day. Both the paper and the radio were filled with talk of some atomic bomb tests in the Marshall Islands. Seems there were aftershocks from the tests that had scientists worried. I'd have to ask the Professor what he thought.

About eleven-thirty I peeked into the lobby and the Professor was there, checking his watch anxiously.

"Are we late, Professor?"

"Mr. Lameroux, there you are! No, we're not late, but I need to get to Madame Narrova's suite early so I can give it the once over. Part of my role as an investigator, you know."

"Well, lead on, MacDuff!"

We took the elevator up to the fourth floor- the penthouse suite. Madame Narrova was getting the full star treatment. Professor Kelley rapped on the door, which was opened immediately by one of Navarro's burly assistants.

"Who dis?" he asked, eyeing me suspiciously.

"This is Marcus," the Professor answered. "He's here to assist me."

Tall, dark and burly moved to the side and we stepped into the suite. A sweet odor wafted through the air. Some kind of incense. The sitting room was buzzing with activity. Professor Kelley hurried off, checking under tables, behind curtains, and whatnot, looking for who knows what. There was a round table in the center of the room, circled by chairs. Izzy Kanamanahounaka, the mayor of Hilo, no less, sat sunk into an overstuffed recliner, nursing some dark concoction in a snifter. A pair of high society couples, dressed in their finest, like they were at a fancy dinner party, chattered away on the couch. A dapper young man wearing a bright Hawaiian shirt sat between the two couples trying not to look out of place. I recognized him as a reporter for the local paper. He'd interviewed me a few days earlier.

Professor Kelley perched on a chair next to a wall, examining the molding with a magnifying glass. A couple of other well-dressed men, vaguely familiar, filled out the attendees. I decided they must be businessmen on vacation. A tall, thin gentleman dressed in an outdated suit mumbled quietly to the burly assistant. But where was the guest of honor?

No sooner had the thought crossed my mind than a new scent filled the air. Expensive perfume. I looked toward the hallway and there she stood, posed dramatically, waiting for everyone to notice. It didn't take long, and the room fell into silence. She was stunning. Dressed alluringly in a blue flowered sarong that made the most of her curvaceous form, her blonde hair falling in curls, she gazed at us with what appeared to me to be amusement. Only when she had our complete attention did she slink into the room. All eyes followed her movements as she glided across the room toward...

Me!

"I don't think we've been introduced," she cooed, her accent captivating.

The Professor hurried to our side.

"I hope you don't mind, Madame Narrova," he said. "This is Marcus Lameroux. I brought him along to assist me."

"Aren't you the band leader, Mr. Lameroux?" she asked.

I had to swallow before I could answer, and my hand reached up to my neck to adjust a necktie before I realized I wasn't wearing one.

"Ahem, well, yes," I stammered. "I am. I hope you don't mind me tagging along with the Professor."

"Not at all," her voice low and husky. "I love your music. So unique."

"Why, thank you, Madame Narrova. That's a great compliment."

Our eyes met for a second, and I swear I would have swooned, if she didn't look away at the last moment. I felt like she was reading me like a book. I've been around the block a few times, seen the world in the service, and women don't usually get the best of me, but standing next to this vixen was intoxicating. Maybe there was something about this gal after all. Glancing at me and giving me a quick smile, she turned gracefully and held out her hands, addressing the room.

"I'm so glad you could all join me tonight. I have a feeling this will be a powerful and enlightening evening for everyone. Why don't we go ahead and get started? Professor, are we ready?"

Kelley's head popped up from behind the bar.

"Oh, yes, everything seems to be in order."

He reached into his jacket pocket and fumbled

with something.

"Fine then, why don't we all sit at the table?"

Everyone rose and gathered around the large round table, jostling for position. After the society ladies and the mayor had been seated the rest of us took our seats. I was situated to the right of one of the ladies, a double string of pearls around her neck and diamonds hanging from her ears. As I made myself comfortable she touched my arm and whispered to me.

"I loved your show, Mr. Lameroux. So exotic! Just the right atmosphere for this wonderful island."

"Thank you, Mrs. -?"

"Vanderpeel."

Mrs. Armand Vanderpeel? I stole a look at her husband, immediately to her left. He was the largest diamond importer in the world. Madame Narrova certainly attracted important clients. I wondered if they had a particular purpose for being here, or if it was just idle curiosity. All eyes were turned toward our host. She looked at each of us in turn before she spoke.

"Let us begin. Please join hands. Josefus, would you get the lights?"

The burly fellow turned down the lights and took his place by the door. The tall man I'd seen earlier was nowhere to be seen. That was suspicious. The only light in the room now came from three candles on the table. I felt Mrs. Vanderpeel's delicate hand grip mine, and on the other side the reporter laid his hand on top of mine.

All eyes were focused on the stunning beauty flanked by Kelley and the Mayor. She closed those gorgeous eyes and took a deep breath. The room was silent, filled with anticipation. After a few moments her lips parted and she spoke with a deep commanding voice.

"The mists are parting. I peer into the world beyond. I see faces. They want to speak. I see a young woman, pale skin, dark hair, and water... something about water..."

Madame Narrova's head twisted at a weird angle and then flopped back. She sat motionless while we all stared. Slowly, ever so slowly, her head lifted and I swear the look in her eyes spooked me. They seemed to shine.

"Katy? Katy, are you there? I can feel you, but I can't see you."

That voice was not Madame Narrova's, or it was unlike any voice I'd heard her use. I'm a skeptic about all this stuff, but I have to admit a chill ran up my spine. There was no trace of Narrova's accent in that voice, and—"Ow!" What was that? Mrs. Vanderpeel was squeezing my hand so hard I thought she would break it.

"Steph... Stephanie?"

It was Mrs. Vanderpeel, and she sounded about ready to burst into tears.

"Oh, Katy! You are there! I've missed you so much!" Madame Narrova said in that weird, high voice.

And then Mrs. Vanderpeel *did* cry.

"Oh Katy, please don't cry. I'm okay. Everything's okay. It's wonderful here. I just miss you and mom and dad."

I remembered reading a profile once on the early life of Mrs. Katherine Vanderpeel. She had a sister who died on a family vacation. She drowned and there was talk of Katherine being implicated. It was all hushed up in the end.

"Please tell mom and dad I'm okay, will ya?"

"I'll tell them Steph," Mrs. Vanderpeel said, sobbing, and then she blurted out, "I love you Steph, I always will..." before she broke down completely.

"I know you do, sis. I love you too. I have to go now. It's hard to talk like this."

Madame Narrova's head fell forward. It had been an impressive performance, full of drama, but all that information was available to anybody. I wasn't convinced. I had to admit she had this crowd in the palm of her hand, though. Slowly she lifted her head, and when we could see her face, we saw her brow was furrowed. Her eyes flashed with anger.

"Money!" she said in that deep, commanding tone. "I sense something about some missing money. A lot of money. It's been taken from somewhere, and hidden."

Well, that was general enough. It could apply to a lot of different things, but when I looked around the circle there was one person who really didn't like what he was hearing. The mayor had turned bright red, and if looks could kill, Madame Narrova would have dropped dead right there.

"Fifty thousand dollars. This money belonged to a lot of people. It was meant for something good," Madame Narrova said. "It's in a cool place. Buried... no, not underground, but under... something, underneath..."

I sensed movement to my right and I noticed the reporter had taken out a pencil and pad, and was writing it all down.

"I'm getting a picture...a house... An expensive house..."

I glanced over at the mayor. His jaw was clenched and he looked about ready to bolt, but just then the room, the entire room *shook.* No, not the room- the entire building. And then again. Earthquake? Living in California I was no stranger to quakes, but this didn't feel quite right. Then my mind flashed back to the news reports of the atomic bomb tests in the Marshall Islands. Could this be somehow related? And then it started to rain- hard. Like it had been switched on, sheets of rain pelted the windows and beat out a frightening rhythm on the roof.

As if that wasn't enough, Narrova let out a strange, strangled cry and fell forward on the table, twitching. Her arms flopped around uncontrollably, and I swear her body undulated. It wobbled in a manner that seemed impossible for something that had bones inside it. This was weird stuff, and I took a deep breath to try and clear my thoughts, and when I did, I smelled the ocean, and I noticed my skin felt wet and clammy. My first thought was that a window had broken, or there was a hole in the roof, but I couldn't see any evidence of that.

Professor Kelley stood next to the psychic, his eyes wide, staring down at her form, and when the room started to glow with an eerie light I saw why. In Madame Narrova's place... no, in the *same* place as her body was a weird blob-like form, like a big jellyfish with a myriad of ugly tentacles flopping around like a fish out of water.

Narrova's mouth opened and closed, like she was gasping for air, and she made strange bubbling noises. Everyone was riveted to their spots, except the Professor, who had pulled a small camera from his jacket, and was snapping pictures in rapid fire succession.

"OPP... GLARG! ... GLUUU..."

Madame Narrova was trying to speak, but she wasn't making much sense. With what seemed like great difficulty, she sat up, that strange image of a jellyfish still superimposed over her body.

"SSSSEA... BELOW... AWAKE... WHY... GLAUC..."

Water dripped from her mouth, more than seemed possible.

"WWWWHO YOU?... WATER... WHY AWAKE...GLAAAA"

The tall man I had seen earlier rushed to Narrova's side, stared at her form for a second, and then grabbed her shoulders, shaking her. It turns out he was her doctor, and as he was charged with maintaining her health, he didn't think this was a very good situation. I had to agree. It seemed to work. Just as suddenly as it came, the vision vanished, and we had Madame Narrova back again. She slumped into the doctor's arms, unconscious. Tall, dark and burly turned on the lights and everyone stood up.

I rushed over the lady's side. Professor Kelley was still snapping pictures.

"Look at this," he whispered to me, pointing out a series of bizarre star shaped welts on her arms.

Had we all just been the victims of a bizarre mass hallucination, or did Madame Narrova turn into a jellyfish for a few minutes? I favored the hallucination theory, but a fine mist still hung in the air, and those welts on her arms were still there.

The lady's eyes flickered open and she looked around as if she was confused.

"What... what happened?" she asked.

"You don't remember?" the professor replied.

"I still see an image of the ocean, deep, deep under the sea, and I feel like I was inside something. Something big."

I noticed she was shivering.

"Doctor Fratalini, could you bring me something? I'm... I'm cold."

The doctor fetched a blanket and wrapped the woman in it. He helped his patient stand up and then turned to us.

"Everyone, Madame must rest. I'm sure you can understand. Her health is very delicate and this excitement has been too much. We can continue at some other time. My apologies."

We bade our goodbyes to Madame and headed for the door, the reporter begging the mayor for a comment as the official practically ran for the exit.

"Come to my room, Marcus. There's something I want to show you," said the professor

We took the elevator to the next floor down and I followed Kelley to his room. Once inside he handed me a piece of paper and a pencil.

"Draw a picture of the marks you saw on Madame Narrova's arms."

Without comment I took the paper and started drawing. While I was busy the professor shuffled through some papers in a briefcase. When I was finished I handed him my drawing, which looked like a lopsided five pointed star with a circle in the center. The professor handed me a couple of photographs. I looked at them and my eyes narrowed in bafflement.

"That first photo is of a drawing made by a fisherman in Chile last year. After a huge earthquake off the coast one of his crew fell overboard. They found him a few days later, with those marks all over his body."

"It looks exactly like what I just drew."

"Look at the next photo. It's a portion of a papyrus scroll found near the Red Sea. It's believed to be over four thousand years old."

I had to swallow a lump in my throat before I could reply.

"Professor Kelley, this also looks like the marks we saw on Narrova's arms. I've never heard of these scrolls. Have you written about them?"

"Not yet. Very few know about them. The scrolls are written in a form of hieroglyphs subtly different from any encountered before. They still haven't been deciphered completely. The last photograph you have is of a rock found off the coast of New Zealand."

I was staring wide eyed at an image of a stone with several of the star shapes running in a straight line across its face.

"We're not sure if those markings were carved in the rock by some ancient civilization, or produced by... other means."

"What do you mean, other means?"

Before the professor could answer an intense sheet of water pounded the window and we both hurried to look outside. It was storming alright- a real lollapalooza. The ocean was churning like a swimming pool after somebody did a cannonball into the water, and it looked like even the largest ships were in danger of capsizing.

"I have more photos just like that from all

corners of the Earth," the professor said. "That's not all. There are reports throughout history, of sightings of immense tentacles, unbelievably long, covered in these unusual star-shaped stingers. Only the tentacles have ever been seen, never the bells or stalks. And it's always after some disturbance- underwater volcano eruptions, earthquakes, tsunamis."

"That's fascinating, Professor. I've never heard of any of this."

"This is a rare phenomena. The sightings are separated by decades, even hundreds of years."

"You mentioned tentacles, bells and stalks. That sounds like what- a jellyfish?"

Professor Kelley smiled at me.

"Yes, exactly. A jellyfish. Or something like a jellyfish. A primal ancestor, perhaps."

"And only the tentacles have been seen? Even in the ancient texts? Are they ripped off during the earthquakes or something?"

"That's one possibility. Another is that the organism is so large only the tentacles can be seen. The rest is so far below the surface it can't be seen."

This was a lot to take in. I stared at the raging storm outside for a minute before I replied.

"Are you telling me there are schools of giant jellyfish roaming around under the oceans?"

Kelley sighed and sat down in the easy chair next to the window.

"Maybe. Or maybe just one. One really, really big specimen that lives on the ocean floor, stretching across the entire planet."

My jaw dropped open. All I could do was stare at the professor. The idea was outrageous.

165

"Jellyfish are the oldest multi-organ animals on the Earth, at least 700 million years old," he said. "There are some scientists who believe the Earth is one giant living organism. If this is true, why not a creature so big it could stretch from one end of the sea to the other?"

He reached into his suit jacket and pulled out a small tape recorder. So that's what I had seen him fumbling with during the séance. He pressed the rewind button for a few seconds and then hit play. We listened for a bit and then Madame Narrova's strange utterances sputtered from the tiny speaker.

"OPP... GLARG! ... GLUUU..."

"Now listen carefully," the Professor said.

"SSSSEA... BELOW... AWAKE... WHY... GLAUC..."

My nerves tingled, remembering that eerie glow in the room, and the water dribbling from the woman's mouth as she slowly formed these words.

"WWWWHO YOU?... WATER... WHY AWAKE...GLAAAA"

Professor Kelley pressed the stop button and looked at me.

"That scroll I mentioned earlier. Part of it has been translated. It mentions a being, ancient even then, that they seemed to fear. They called it the Sleeper Under the Sea. And then there are the Maphuche legends from Chile. They sacrifice animals, even people, to the sea- or something in the sea, in order to keep things in balance. They still do it. Earlier this year a young boy was thrown in the sea after a tsunami."

"But you're talking about thousands of years. How could something live that long?" I asked.

The professor raised his finger in the air, a light

166

in his eyes.

"That's the question, isn't it? Nothing on the Earth lives that long. Or nothing from this Earth."

Okay, that was it. I respected the professor, but this stuff he was talking about was way out there. This was just about all I could handle.

"Professor, this is too much. My brain is fried. I need to get some sleep. Thanks for a very interesting evening. I'll catch up with you later."

I could see the disappointment in Kelley's eyes as he showed me to the door. I stumbled down the hall toward my own room. I hadn't realized how exhausted I was. I was still trying to make sense of everything when my eyes mercifully flickered shut and I plummeted into deep sleep, the rain pounding at my window.

When I woke up the rain was still pounding. No, that wasn't the rain, someone was pounding on my door.

"Lameroux, are you in there? Open the door!"

Oh great, it was Greenberg. What time was it? Had I missed a show? The clock on the nightstand said ten after twelve, and light was coming through the window, so it was just past noon. The pounding got louder.

"Lameroux, wake up!"

"I'm coming," I whined, dragging myself to the door.

I fumbled with the lock and pulled the door open. Greenberg looked perturbed, but then, he always did.

"What?" I grumbled.

"It's this rain. It hasn't stopped since last night, and it doesn't look like it's going to any time soon. Some kind of freak storm. Nobody can go outside, so everyone's cooped up in their rooms or the lounge. They're upset. Ruined vacations, all that kind of crap. I need you and the boys to do a show right now. Not the big dinner show, just some quiet music to calm people down and give them something to focus on."

"Extra show, extra money," I said, looking him straight in his cold, beady eyes.

"Yeah, I figured you'd say that. Start in ten minutes."

"We'll be there in half an hour," I said, swinging the door shut.

Looking out the window as I dressed, I could see why no one wanted to go outside. It was a mess. The smaller boats had been pulled up on the shore and turned over. The larger craft had been covered as best they could be, to prevent them from filling with rain. The waves still pummeled the shoreline, threatening to wash everything out to sea. Hurriedly I finished dressing and went to roust the rest of the band.

The boys were a little groggy, and so was I, and we didn't have the dancers, so we played a low-key set, which seemed to suit the audience. Some were visibly upset by the endless pounding of the rain. Word was going around that the phone lines were out, and roads were washed out too, so we really were trapped here. The storm had gotten so intense some of the boats had disappeared from the dock. We skipped the snappy numbers and played our softer repertoire, things we usually saved for last call.

I spotted the professor at a table in the back, scribbling in a notebook, every once in a while thumbing through a couple of old books. Things were going pretty well, and the crowd was calming down when a huge wind shook the building and the lights dimmed for a few seconds. The vacationers who weren't too potted looked around nervously and Greenberg rushed up onto the stage. I signaled for the band to hush and stepped away from the mic.

"Ladies and gentlemen," Greenberg said, out of breath. "We're sorry for this inconvenience, but don't worry. If the power does go out, our emergency generators are ready and waiting. Please make yourselves at home. Now, back to the exquisite song stylings of Marcus Lameroux and His Hwaiian-aires."

He gestured toward the band and rushed off the stage, his face red. This must be a nightmare for him. After a few more numbers we took a break and I headed for Kelly's table. Before I could say anything the professor gestured for me to sit down.

"We're having another séance," he said. "Are you in?"

"Me? Why are you asking me?"

"Madame Narrova seems to like you. It might help if you're there." He picked up the book. "I've been doing some research on the Sleeper Under the Sea and I'm convinced it has something to do with this storm. I want to try and contact it."

This all sounded like hogwash to me, but I wasn't going to pass up another chance to see the European vixen in action, fake or not. I had to admit she was intoxicating.

"Okay professor, I'll be there."

I led the band through one more desultory set before I let them go. They were nervous about the storm themselves, so I wanted to give them some time to let off steam in whatever way they might choose. Besides, I needed some shuteye. As I headed for my room the wind shook the building again. If this went on much longer the power lines were sure to go down. I hoped the generators were as reliable as Greenberg said they were.

When I woke up that evening the rain was pounding against the windows in my room so mercilessly I was afraid they'd shatter. That meant everyone had been inside all day. Nerves were sure to be on edge. The lounge was filled to capacity in anticipation of our evening show. There was nowhere else to go. The boys were on edge just as much as the crowd.

I decided to use that energy and start the show with a bang. On my cue the boys launched into the Hawaiian War Chant. Nate, our drummer, was no Buddy Rich, but he could pound those skins pretty tight. When he got into his duet with Bartella on vibes they really got cooking, and the crowd was loving it. Finally, the hula dancers sashayed in, double time, and the rubes were all smiles. The boys were having a good time too, I could tell. Everyone needed this. Having been cooped up inside all day, instead of enjoying the sun and sand was not good for morale, and they needed to let off a little steam.

I motioned for Silverman to take his place at the mic, and I joined him. Together we launched into the vocals.-

"Kaua i ka huahua'i. E `uhene la'i pili ko'olua."

The Hawaiian was a little tricky to learn, but once you got it down, it was a lot of fun. It was a bit of hokum. The song was originally a love song, not a chant, but the crowd was loving it, and by the time we got to the "au-wayyyy" part they were singing along. I signaled the boys to let us sing it through again, and by the time we finished people were dancing. I even spotted Greenberg in a corner, smiling and nodding his head.

Our music had worked its charms. We'd changed the mood of the room, and when we finished that number I knew we could move into our more serene material, and all would be fine. I called for "Sweet Leilani" and couples moved close, slow dancing. Silverman chimed in with his frogs and bird calls, and everything was fine. Now if that rain and wind would just let up.

The rest of the evening was smooth sailing, except every time the building shook from the wind. I could see nervous eyes scan the ceiling, and I must admit I didn't much care for it either. We knocked off about ten and the boys split for who knows where. I suspected there was a card game going on somewhere. The crowd seemed in good spirits, hunkering up to the bar, or ordering late night nosh. I wondered how long the larder could last without getting more supplies. A local teenage boy sat on the edge of the stage strumming tunes on a ukulele.

I found Professor Kelly in the lobby, staring out a window and wringing his hands.

"Pardon my French, Professor, but this rain is a real pain in the ass," I said.

His eyes met mine and he said, "The duration and intensity of this storm is highly unusual. The mayor says he can't remember a storm like this in his lifetime."

As if to punctuate his remark a flash of lightning lit up the window, followed immediately by a clap of thunder so loud it got everyone's attention, and then the building shook. I wasn't cold, but I couldn't stop myself from shivering.

"Are you ready?" the Professor asked. "We're getting started right away."

"Right now? Sure, I'm game."

I followed Kelly up to Madame Narrova's suite. The whole time he babbled on about atmospheric pressure, oceanographic phenomena, psychic forces and ancient legends. I was too distracted to follow what he was saying. It was all mumbo jumbo to me, and the building shakes seemed to be getting more frequent.

Tall, dark and gruesome let us into Narrova's suite. The only other ones inside were her doctor, the mayor and Madame herself. There was no showy costume this time. She was dressed simply in black Capri slacks and a form-fitting top. Still stunning. This then was not to be an exhibition for clients. The lady rose and glided toward us. I had to admit she had grace to spare. She took the professor's hands in hers.

"Professor Kelly," was all she said, a grim look on her face.

She held out one delicate hand to me and smiled. My heart jumped, involuntarily. She wanted me to reach out to her. I obliged.

"Thank you for coming, Mr. Lameroux. Though I sense you are not a believer, I also sense an inner balance in you that I appreciate. I think it may help me stay centered tonight."

"Thank you, Madame Narrova, that's a great compliment, but I'm afraid I don't feel very balanced at this moment," I grinned.

She returned my smile and gave my hand a little

squeeze before letting go. Such close contact with this exotic beauty made my head spin and I blurted out something I probably shouldn't have.

"Mayor, I'm surprised to see you here, after that hasty exit last night."

The mayor drew himself up to his full height and squared his shoulders, defiantly looking in my eyes.

"Despite the, um, allegations, or should I say, inferences that were made in this room at a previous time, I am Mayor of this city, and I take that responsibility very seriously. This storm may threaten the safety of my community, and if there's anything that can be done here tonight to alleviate that danger, I wish to take part in those efforts."

I blushed and looked at the floor.

"I'm sorry, Mayor. No offense intended."

Just then a sheet of rain hit the window with a noisy smack, capturing everyone's attention, letting me off the hook.

"Shall we get started, Madame?" the professor asked.

"Yes, thank you, Professor Kelly. I've been having disturbing visions all day. Will you all have a seat at the table?"

"What kind of visions?" I asked, as everyone present took a chair. To my great delight I found myself seated next to Madame Narrova, on her left. The doctor was seated on her right.

"I guess I shouldn't call them visions," Madame Narrova replied as she lit the candles in the center of the table. "They're just impressions, sensations. I keep hearing the sound of an explosion, but it's muffled, like it's coming from a long way away, or maybe the sound is traveling through water. And it gets hard to breathe, like I'm drowning. And then confusion. Why am I there? What's happening? I'm reaching out, trying to grab something, anything, but it's hard to move, and there's nothing within reach. The whole world is shaking. Then it all fades away, and I'm back. I have been communicating with the spirit realm for quite some time, but this is different. Whatever I've been feeling, it's not in the spirit realm. It hasn't passed over. It's alive."

She glanced around the table, and to my eye she looked scared. Whatever it was, dreams, visions, whatever, it had her spooked.

"Everyone please join hands," she said.

"Madame Narrova, I know this may be difficult, but could you please attempt to contact the creature that appeared here last night?" Professor Kelly instructed.

Narrova took a deep breath, looked at the professor and her lip trembled slightly. I could imagine inside she was screaming, "No! Please, I don't want to." But to her credit her reply was simply, "I will try."

She closed her eyes, sat motionless for a moment, and then her head slumped forward. Her breathing grew heavy, uneven, and her hand tightened around mine. The lady had quite a grip. Her head rose, eyes still closed and her mouth opened and closed, like she was gasping for air. We all sat transfixed. After a moment sounds came from her mouth, soft, hard to make out.

"... uhh... fsssh... wa...wa..." was all I could make out.

Then, suddenly, a flash of lightning, a crash of thunder, and Madame's body stiffened. She squeezed my hand so hard I winced. I looked over at the doctor and his hand was getting the same treatment. Too much of this and I wouldn't be playing the guitar anytime soon. Her eyes sprang open, wide, staring, but focused somewhere beyond the walls of this room.

"GUH...GUH...WUH..." she babbled, and then, "WHY? WHY... AM I... HERE? ...GUH... WHERE IS?"

And then, I swear to God, this *thing* appeared. A glowing, shimmering shape, a luminescent glob, undulating like a bag full of water, formed around Madame Narrova's body. Her hand, still squeezing mine so hard it had cut off the circulation in my fingers, turned icy cold.

"WHAT?... WA...WHAT?" she moaned.

Slow, wavelike shapes were running down the length of the glowing glob, and now weird tentacles were forming. There were at least a dozen of them, snaking through the air. One came straight at me and I braced myself for whatever weird sensation it would bring, but it went right through me.

"Everyone, keep holding hands. Don't break the circle," Professor Kelly said.

The mayor looked like he wanted to bolt, but everyone stayed put. The tentacles wiggled around in the air, perhaps searching for something, anything to grab onto.

"SH... SH... SHAKING... EVERYTHING. ALL AROUND... SHAKING."

"Who are you?" the professor asked. "Why are you here?"

Madame Narrova's head jerked toward Kelly, but her wide eyes were still glazed, unseeing. The glowing blob surrounding her body convulsed.

"SOUND... WHAT?... AWAKE... I... AWAKE..."

"You're awake. Something has awakened you. Is that what you mean?"

The blob shape pulsated violently, the tentacles waved frantically, and the lady let loose with the loudest scream I'd ever heard. She sounded like someone stuck a hot poker through her. My ears were ringing and my heart just about jumped out of my throat. I don't mind saying I had the willies.

There was another enormous clap of thunder, and with a tremendous crash, a tree branch shattered the window. The storm had grown so violent it was ripping trees apart. A sheet of icy water exploded into the room, and to top it off the lights went out.

"The power lines have gone down!" the mayor shouted, barely audible over the pounding rain.

Narrova twisted quickly and got loose from my grip, falling to the floor. Her body flopped and flailed, arms shaking, while the shape around her beat with a primal rhythm, the tentacles slithering across the floor.

"What's going on, professor?" I shouted.

"It's the Sleeper Under the Sea. Something has awakened it from its unending slumber. It's causing these storms!" After a second he added, "This is not good!"

Just then the lights came on. God bless Greenberg and his generators. They didn't stop what was happening on the floor, though. Madame Narrova moaned and started gibbering.

"WA...WA...WHAT...   NOISE...
SHAKE...WORLD... SHAKE..."

The doctor stood over his charge, unsure of what he should do. Lightning flashed. Thunder rent the air. The building shook harder than ever. Things were desperate. Something had to happen fast. In a flash I had an idea. It was crazy, but nobody else was offering any solutions.

"Professor, I think I can help, but I'm going to need some assistance. Give me a few minutes to round up some of the boys. While I'm gone, see if you and Josefus can cover up that window somehow."

"Okay, Marcus, but hurry up!"

As I ran out the door, I glanced back at the figure thrashing around on the floor. I hoped like hell this worked. With the auxiliary generators running, I didn't trust the elevator, so I headed for the service stairway and bolted down to the third floor. Reaching the hallway, the building shook again and the lights dimmed briefly. It was chaos. The picture window at the far end of the hallway had shattered and the carpet was soaked, littered with debris. People milled about, either chased from their rooms by the elements or roused by the commotion, and there was Greenberg, doing his best to placate his guests, urging them to congregate in the lobby for free drinks. He was a lousy boss, but I had to hand it to him; the hospitality business was his true calling.

I pushed my way through the crowd to Silverman's door and pounded as hard as I could. It took a minute, but he finally answered, bleary eyed. Christ, how could he sleep through this?

"Marcus, what is it?"

"Mel, there's no time to explain. We have an emergency. Roust as many of the boys as possible and meet me upstairs at Madame Narrova's suite. Have them bring their instruments."

"But, what-"

"No time. Really, just do it," I called as I made my way down the hallway toward Greenberg.

There was an enormous crash of thunder and the building shook again, so hard I nearly lost my footing.

"Please, Mr. and Mrs. Giddings, I know it's a terrible imposition, but any damage will be compensated. Please join us in the lobby until the storm dies down for complimentary cocktails. It's on the house."

He was doing his best, but the look on Greenberg's face was grim. I made it to his side and clutched his arm.

"Greenberg, is it true you have a Hammond organ here?"

He gave me a look like I was asking him if he had a UFO. I suppose that organ was the farthest thing from his mind at the moment. He finally managed a slow and confused reply.

"Yes... but it hasn't been used in years."

"Where is it?"

"What do you want it for? This is no-"

"No time. Just tell me where it is!"

"It's in a storage room behind the stage."

"Is it locked?"

"No, there isn't even a door on the room, just a curtain over the doorway."

"Thank you!" I shouted, and sprinted down the stairs.

The scene in the lobby wasn't nearly as chaotic as the hallway above. Greenberg's crew was doing a good job of placating unhappy tourists. A few were trying to tune into something, anything, on the radio, but they couldn't raise much except static.

Alcohol was flowing freely, but how long would the supply hold out? A sheet of plywood was affixed to the front door. A branch must have crashed through.

I made my way through the lounge, dimly lit and abandoned, into the backstage area, located the storage room and pushed the curtain aside. Nothing much could be seen in the ambient light, but I found a switch and flipped it. The room was dusty but not as bad as it could have been. Towards the back, behind several rows of boxes of restaurant supplies was what I was looking for. Sheltered beneath a sheet was the Hammond B3, and it was in pretty good shape. Fortunately it was a spinet model, so I wouldn't have to find an amp and speaker.

I wheeled it out of the store room toward the lobby and realized there was no way to get it to Madame Narrova's suite except for the elevator. I'd have to chance it. Pushing the instrument into the elevator I pressed the button marked 4 and hoped for the best. The car lurched slightly and slowly rose. I heard thunder through the walls and held my breath for the rest of the ride.

On the third floor the car stopped and the door slid open. There stood the figure of a young woman, wearing a long caftan, soaked to the bone, dripping wet, her blond hair plastered flat against her body. She looked like a little kitten that accidentally jumped in the bathtub. I recognized her. It was Nate, the drummer's girlfriend. She rushed into the elevator and fell into my arms.

"Oh, Mr. Lameroux, I've been looking everywhere for you!" she sobbed.

"What is it, dear?" I asked, instinctively

wrapping my arms around her.

"It's... it's Nate."

She was crying so hard she could barely speak.

"What is it? What about Nate?"

"He... he's gone..."

"Gone? Where?"

She trembled, as I wasn't sure if it was from the hysterics or because she was drenched.

"He wanted to go out on the beach and get some shells. I told him it wasn't a good idea, because of the storm and all, but he said it would be romantic, so I went with him. I didn't want him going out there all by himself, you know?'

She looked up at me and burst into tears. I held her tighter.

"Yes, yes... what happened then?"

"He found a couple shells, so I said let's go back Nate, we're getting soaked. We're right out there on the beach, next to the water, and he says no, come on, we can get a few more. I had a hold of his arm, and I tried to pull him back, but he pulled away from me. And then... and then..."

She completely lost it, burying her face in my chest. I patted her on the back.

"And then what, Sal? And then what?"

"And then this thing came up out of the water. It was like a long cable, or a rope, or giant snake or something, and it wrapped around Nate, and it *took him.*"

"What do you mean, it took him?"

She was crying again and I had to shake her before she could answer.

"It... it just went back into the water, and it dragged Nate with it. I watched for a minute, but I was so scared, Mr. Lameroux. I ran back here and

I've been looking for you. We've got to try and find him! He's out there, Mr. Lameroux. You've got to do something!"

I pushed her away and looked her straight in the eye.

"Listen, Sal, this is crazy talk. You need to get a hold of yourself. There's nothing we can do tonight in this rain. Go back down to the lobby. Have a drink. Have a few. I'll meet you down there as soon as I can. Right now there's something important I need to do."

"More important than Nate?" she asked, straightening up for the first time.

"I'll explain later," I said, helping her into the hallway and pressing the button to the fourth floor. As the door slid closed I could see the look of disbelief and anger on her face.

I had no doubt everything she said was true, which made my mission even more urgent. Just as the car started to rise everything shook, The car slowed down but kept going. I took a deep breath and said a little prayer. Normally I'm not a religious person, but things were getting crazy. And I really needed to get to the fourth floor with this organ.

When the elevator door slid open I let myself breath again. I'd made it. There stood Melvin Silverman and Maselli with his flute and didgeridoo, staring at me. That was it? No drums, no percussion at all, no vibes. Considering what I had in mind, maybe that was best.

"Where's everybody else?" I asked, pushing the organ into the hallway. "Where's Bartella?"

"I could only find Phil," Silverman said. "What's going on? Weird noises are coming from

Narrova's suite."

"Gentlemen, we have a job to do. A command performance. You were both there when things got weird at KONG-Tiki. Things are about to get weird again. Steel yourselves and follow me."

I pushed the Hammond into Madame Narrova's suite and stopped dead in my tracks. Behind me I heard Silverman let out a low whistle. The bloated, bubbling blob in the middle of the room had doubled in size since I left and I could barely see Narrova's figure inside of it. Her voice was muffled but I could still hear it. She had gone from babbling incoherently to flat out screaming bloody murder. I don't know what happened inside her mind when she was in a trance, but she had to be close to insanity. The misty tentacles still groped in the air, seeking something, anything.

The mayor was pressed against the far wall, a terrified look on his face. The doctor and the bodyguard both looked lost, helpless. They were supposed to be protecting the woman but there was absolutely nothing they could do. Professor Kelly stood next to one of the ropy arms, taking pictures.

"Marcus, thank goodness you're back," he said. "What have you got in mind?"

"Professor, we're going to play that thing a little lullaby."

I found a wall socket, plugged in the organ and pressed the on switch. It would take a minute to warm up. Kelly's eyes widened and a smile came over his face. Holding down the switch, I pressed the run switch at the same time.

"Silverman, can you do waves? Like the sound of waves gently lapping against the shore? And bubbles- bubbles rising through the water?"

"I can make any sound you name. No problem."

Thunder, loud. The wind howled through the makeshift covering over the broken window.

"We need to put that thing over there to sleep, so we're going to play it the most soothing music we can. No rhythm, no melody, just sound, long, low, and quiet. Follow my lead."

I pressed a couple of the keys on the organ. There was a soft thunk, and then nothing. I tried again. Same thing. Greenberg said this thing hadn't been used in years. Hell, what if it didn't work? I grabbed the back panel and yanked. It took a bit of work but I got it off. The inside was littered with clumps of grass, leaves, chewed up paper. Christ, it was full of rat's nests, and the tone wheels couldn't turn. I tore frantically at the mess, clearing out all the detritus. If I couldn't get this thing working we were in a lot of trouble.

Back at the keyboard I pressed a couple of notes. With the back open I could hear the tone wheels start to turn, and then came the low, rich rumble that only came from a Hammond. Thank goodness. I set the drawbars for a classic Jimmy Smith sound and pressed the lowest foot pedal. Smooth tones filled the air. I smiled.

"Silverman, you stand next to that thing over there and do your best to sound like a calm ocean day. There's a lady inside there and I want her to hear you."

Mel looked at the glowing blob and then back at me, a worried look on his face, but he stepped up and nodded. I played a low C chord and held it for a full thirty seconds, adding two bass foot pedals, before going up a half octave and slowly playing a sweeping flourish. Maselli joined in, playing a pure low C on his flute that harmonized perfectly with what I was laying down, and held the note longer than I thought humanly possible. He read my intent. Pure sound. Get that thing's attention and lull it to sleep. Silverman started in with his sounds and when I closed my eyes I could swear I was on the beach on a calm summer day.

We went on like that for three or four minutes, holding every note twice as long as we should, and the music was starting to make sense. Maselli and I were in a groove. It was soothing. That's when I noticed the tentacles. They were contracting. I resisted the impulse to jump off my bench and shout with joy. It was working. After five minutes the screaming stopped. I hoped that was a good sign.

And then... that thing started making the weirdest noise I'd ever heard. It was a wailing, moaning kind of a sound, warbling in a low register. When Maselli and I went up a note, that thing did too, and I knew what was going on. Dear God, that thing was singing along with us! I made a round shape with my hand and held it up to my mouth. Maselli knew the signal. He put his flute down and picked up the didgeridoo. When he blew the first blast on the instrument the glob went silent.

I let Maselli take the lead, blowing impossibly long, low notes, while I faded into the background, holding extended chords that filled in the space around his breath breaks. That man had the most amazing breath control I'd ever witnessed. He deserved a raise. It was when Silverman looked back at me and gave me a thumbs up that I noticed. The thing was shrinking.

Soon Madame Narrova's form was easily seen through the jellyfishes translucent skin. We kept up our drone for another twenty minutes. I don't know how Maselli kept it up, but he did, and in one specific moment the ghostly sea creature simply blinked out of existence. I signaled Maselli and Silverman to stop. We just sat there, exhausted. Nobody moved.

"Do you hear it?" Kelly whispered.

"What?" I asked. I was too emotionally drained to think.

"Silence."

It dawned on me what he was saying. No thunder. No howling wind. No *rain*. He padded across the room and shook my hand.

"You did it. You boys did it. You put it to sleep. I don't want to overstate things here, but you may have just saved the lives of everyone on this island, and maybe..."

"She's okay! She's okay!"

It was the doctor, kneeling at Madame Narrova's side, taking her pulse.

"She's just sleeping."

***

We heard on the radio later that there had been terrible storms, hurricanes, even a tsunami, all throughout the Pacific. Australia, North and South America had all been affected. There was speculation that the offshore nuclear bomb tests had somehow been connected. It's true, they had, but not in the way the scientists thought. Kelly and I knew though. Those bombs shook the Earth, deep down below the surface, and awakened something that sleeps down there, has been sleeping for uncounted eons. It woke up and all hell broke loose. The boys and I, we put it back to sleep, and at the same time, on that night in 1960 we created what came to be known as New Age music.

As soon as the rain stopped, people were anxious to get outside. They combed the beach, littered with seaweed, dead fish, torn branches, all manner of garbage, and one body. They found Nate's bloated body washed up on the shore not far from the hotel. Poor Sal was inconsolable. Nate was one hell of a drummer and a swell guy. It was a terrible loss. Nobody knew what to make of the odd star shaped markings that covered his body. Nobody but me and Professor Kelly.

One thing I couldn't understand. How had this thing caused such havoc across such a large area?

"I told you before," Kelly told me. "This specimen may reach across the entire planet. In fact- it may *be* the planet. Have you ever heard of the Gaia Theory? Some people believe the planet is one giant living organism."

I didn't want to think about that. This thing had lain on the bottom of the ocean, sleeping, since the beginning of time. We'd awakened it with our meddling. The world was getting noisier by the day. Jet planes, traffic rumble, nuclear bomb testing, even music was getting noisier all the time. One thought filled me with dread to my soul- how would we stop the Sleeper Under the Sea if it woke up again?

ABOUT THE AUTHOR

Lee Widener first wanted to be a cowboy, then an astronaut, then a rock n roll musician. None of that happened. Then he wanted to be a writer. That happened. Along the way he did a lot of theatre, ran several internet radio stations, drew a lot of silly pictures, and had some fiction published. His Bizarro novella ROCK N ROLL HEAD CASE was published by Eraserhead Press in 2015. Some of the stories in this book have been published before. Some of them are new.

Made in the USA
Middletown, DE
05 December 2020